These were perplexing questions

Did Clint know his brother was acquainted with her late husband? Jocelyn's instincts told her he did. But why hadn't he told her so? She'd wondered why Clint had taken such an interest in her investigation of Philip's past. Now she had a feeling that Clint was part of that past somehow.

She would have liked to tell herself she was being paranoid. Yet who was Clint Conti really? She knew almost nothing about him. She had shared with him the agonizing experiences of the past few days. She had even entertained lustful thoughts of him. Now she suspected she had made a terrible mistake. So much deception! Her head rang with it.

ABOUT THE AUTHOR

This is Alice Orr's fourth Intrigue novel, the third set in her native northern New York State. She now lives in New York City, where she is president of Alice Orr Literary Agency, wife of Jonathan, mother of grown children, and an avid camper (in the wilds of northwest Jersey) whenever she can find the time. You may write to Alice in care of Alice Orr Agency, Inc., 305 Madison Avenue, Suite 1166, New York, NY 10165. She would love to hear from you.

Books by Alice Orr

HARLEQUIN INTRIGUE
56–SABOTAGE
169–PAST SINS
216–COLD SUMMER

Don't miss any of our special offers. Write to us at the following address for information on our newest releases.

Harlequin Reader Service
901 Fuhrmann Blvd., P.O. Box 1397, Buffalo, NY 14240
Canadian address: P.O. Box 603,
Fort Erie, Ont. L2A 5X3

Camp Fear

Alice Orr

Harlequin Books

TORONTO • NEW YORK • LONDON
AMSTERDAM • PARIS • SYDNEY • HAMBURG
STOCKHOLM • ATHENS • TOKYO • MILAN
MADRID • WARSAW • BUDAPEST • AUCKLAND

To my husband, Jonathan—
always my romantic hero.

To my agents—
Ling Lucas, who is also my dear friend.
Ed Vesneske, who is also my dear son.

To my editor—
Julianne Moore, a true jewel.

ISBN 0-373-22266-1

CAMP FEAR

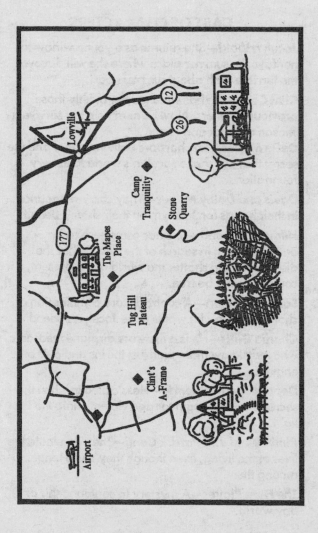

CAST OF CHARACTERS

Jocelyn Wald—She returns as a young widow to her favorite summer place where she will discover the terrible truth about summers past.

Clint Conti—He has watched her quietly those previous summers. Now he must help her survive a season of shock and terror.

DeDe Mapes—She harbors both the anger and the secret that will shake Jocelyn's world to its very foundation.

Davis and Dolby Mapes—They carry vengeance in their hearts for Jocelyn, on their sister's behalf.

Hildy Hammond—She has come here as an anthropologist in search of the past. What she discovers could shatter the world of the present, if it could possibly be true.

Sonny Shannon—A contradictory combination of charm and fury, he wants to be Jocelyn's friend.

Charlie Gillis—He is a first-rate airplane mechanic who may know more than just the ins and outs of engines.

Deputy Sheriff Roemer—He is called in when the secrets and lies begin to rage violently into the light.

Philip Wald and Patrick Conti—They dominate the lives of the living, even though they're no longer among them.

The Flute Player—A mystery to confound this or any world.

Prologue

Jocelyn Wald told herself she wasn't lost. This unmarked road had to meet something with a route sign eventually. Northern New York State was like that. She'd driven here enough last summer and the summer before to know. Unfortunately, in all those explorations she had missed this particular road somehow. She wasn't even sure how she'd gotten onto it this afternoon.

What she'd had in mind was to avoid the usual route north from Syracuse and the painful memories of Philip that went with it. She had made that drive so many times in the two summers past. Philip had been alive then and still her husband. Jocelyn didn't care to be reminded that he was no longer either of those things.

So, today she hadn't taken Route 81 straight to Pulaski, New York. Instead, she veered off that double two-lane interstate and let her own sense of direction take her north along secondary roads—some, such as this one, not even on the map. She had expected to come across familiar bits of landscape by now, but she didn't recognize a thing. She'd been on the road long enough to be in at least the general vicinity of her destination . . . unless as she suspected, she had gone very wrong somehow.

Approaching a turn to the left, she could already tell that that road was wider than the one she was on. That probably meant it led to some place of significance. Jocelyn took the turn and hoped she wasn't headed back where she just came from.

Less than a mile from the junction, she spotted a heartening sight, a roadside fresh produce stand. The structure was little more than a lean-to, sagging at a precarious angle away from its center. The wood was worn and gray and deeply splintered. This might have been a country parody of a city-corner bus shelter if it weren't for the tell-tale shelf that stretched across the front opening. The contents of that shelf would vary from month to month over the summer. Jocelyn anticipated what might be there now—early tomatoes, summer squash and root vegetables that had been stored in a cellar since last fall.

As she drew abreast of the stand, she was surprised at how little was actually on display. A few spindly green and yellow squash, even fewer winter onions and potatoes in small, wooden slatted baskets. That was all. Usually, these places were brimming over this time of year. Either this stand was exceptionally popular and had sold out almost everything in stock, or it was barely making it because it had so little stock to sell. Jocelyn guessed the latter when she saw the two slack-jawed fellows on duty behind the counter. They followed with their eyes as she passed, but otherwise registered no evidence of seeing her or anything else.

Jocelyn had heard of families in these back hills of Lewis County who didn't pay taxes or send their children to school. Local legend claimed folks around here kept shotguns loaded and waiting for a visit from the government or the truant officer, and they didn't welcome other strangers, either. A glance into the faces at the vegetable stand made her wonder if there might be some truth to those stories. She was beyond the stand and heading up a small hill when a blur of motion at the shoulder of the road caught her eye.

"Oh, my God!" she exclaimed and jerked the wheel hard to the right.

She was driving Philip's car, the one he used to take everywhere, because it was a big luxury model that would hold lots of supplies. Now, she wished she were behind the wheel of her more maneuverable compact. The blur was actually a woman. As Jocelyn struggled to veer away she realized that the woman wasn't trying to avoid being hit by the car, she was running toward it.

She was in her midtwenties or maybe older. She had on jeans and a T-shirt. Her long, wildly disheveled hair obscured her face. Nonetheless, there was no hiding her anger. She had her hand raised in a fist, which she was shaking directly at Jocelyn. The car window was open on the driver's side, and she could hear the woman's shouts as well as what she was shouting.

"That's not your car," she screamed. "It's mine. It should be mine."

She continued on her headlong track toward the car she had apparently mistaken for some other vehicle. Jocelyn wasn't about to stop and set the record straight. She had caught only a flashing glimpse of the face behind the straggling hair, and there was more rage there than Jocelyn cared to confront at the moment. Then the first stone hit the window on the passenger's side. This person was actually attacking Jocelyn's car.

She swerved onto the gravel at the edge of the macadam just in time to keep from colliding with her assailant. A rain of stone fragments hit the rear fender on the passenger's side and not just from the spinning of the tires on the loose shoulder. That crazy woman was peppering the car with gravel.

Jocelyn tromped on the accelerator and surged back onto the road. She could see the woman in the rearview mirror. She was still punching the air over her head with one fist while she scooped up more ammunition from the shoulder with the other. Jocelyn corrected the swerve of the car and aimed it down the road at a faster speed than she would otherwise go.

She felt like a coward running away. She could have stopped to explain that there had to be some mistake. This was her car, and the woman was simply confused. Remembering her face in the rearview mirror, Jocelyn suspected that this woman was afflicted with more than confusion. Her soul had been twisted by some far darker influence.

Ordinarily, Jocelyn would have been curious about what the real story behind this bizarre incident might be. However, at the moment her heart was beating hard and her hands gripped the wheel and all she could think about was getting away from this place as rapidly as Philip's big old Lincoln could carry her.

Chapter One

Jocelyn's prayers were answered when her headlong escape from the crazed woman near the vegetable stand ended at a junction with a road Jocelyn recognized. From there on, the trip to the trailer camp was uneventful, except for the trembling in her hands that made her grip the wheel with uncommon tightness all the way.

Camp Tranquility had always felt like home. She usually eased up on the gas pedal the last few miles to enjoy the scenery and fully appreciate her escape from city life. Today, she didn't slow down till she got there. Tranquility had never looked as good to her as it did this afternoon. She didn't really calm down until she reached the campsite she and Philip had rented for the past two seasons.

The scent of pine and grasses toasted by sun reminded Jocelyn that this was the perfect place for her on this or any summer weekend, when she most needed a respite from Syracuse. She and Philip had lived in Syracuse for the five years they'd been married, and on idle weekends memories struck hard. Granted, Camp Tranquility held more startling memories, but shade trees swayed in the easy breeze, Jocelyn listened to the birds and the playful squeals of children cavorting in the pool down the hill, and she felt oddly at peace.

No wonder she couldn't bring herself to cancel the lease for this summer. She couldn't decide to keep it, either. After the way last season ended for her, Bonnie and Joe Delaney, the campground owners, hadn't pushed the issue. They said they understood what Jocelyn must be going through and she could take however long she needed to make up her mind. Bonnie and Joe were like that. They both had good heads for business, but they had good hearts, as well.

Still, Jocelyn hadn't stopped at the split-log office on her way in to the campsite, and not only because she was shaken by her experience back on the road. She knew how kind the Delaneys could be, speaking to Jocelyn gently and smiling with a shadow of melancholy in their eyes, the way so many people had tended to do in the ten months since Philip's death. Nearly everybody treated her as if she needed to be wrapped in cotton wool and not subjected to anything more jarring than hushed voices and delicate movements.

Jocelyn was doing her best to emerge from that fragile state. She had passed the off-kilter stage of shock and grieving disbelief months ago. She wasn't quite sure where that passage had left her, especially given the strange feelings she'd been having lately. She was sure, however, that she didn't care to be swathed in cotton wool this afternoon, no matter how well meant the effort might be. She was certain of this, that is, till the car engine stilled and she opened the door to step outside.

Maybe it was the way the grass looked on the site, as if no one had walked here in a very long time. The Delaneys kept it mowed, of course. Still, there were overgrown patches under the picnic table, where normally the clumps would be flattened out. Obviously, nobody had sat there to sip a beer or wolf down a fire-black hot dog for many months. A feeling of absence pervaded the campsite, like the gray pall of a room too long without heat in a chilly autumn. That absence echoed in Jocelyn's heart with a hollow ache. She was tempted to get back into the car and save this for another day, or perhaps for never.

Philip would have expected her to do exactly that. Philip had made certain assumptions about Jocelyn. He had thought of her as a bit weak in the character department. Jocelyn never challenged those assumptions, not with much vehemence, anyway. She hadn't believed that was the right way to respond. She and Philip had fallen into a pattern, the kind that became habit between married people, like track marks worn into a path.

Jocelyn was determined not to travel that rutted road any longer, now that Philip was gone. She shut the car door behind her and hurried to unlock the trailer before she could think again about how much easier it would be to run away and not give a damn whether the spirit of Philip might be shaking its head knowingly in her wake.

THE REST of the afternoon was too busy for dwelling on morbid thoughts of Philip or of what had happened on the way here. The thirty-six-foot trailer had acquired a layer of dust over the past year, and Jocelyn set to work removing it. She stocked cupboards with the groceries she'd carried north in the big Lincoln and put out fresh linens. By evening, her home away from home was cozy and comfortable.

Night fell, accompanied by the chorus of woodland sounds that Jocelyn had always loved. Unfortunately, they didn't sound so comforting tonight. She had been by herself here often, but this was the first time she had ever felt alone. In the past there had been the prospect of Philip's turning up eventually, acting as a buffer between her and any threat the darkness might hold. Tonight, there would be no husband driving down the slope to poke his shamed face in at the trailer door with some excuse or other for being later than promised. Maybe that was why she could feel the skin pulling tense along her arms and on the back of her neck. Or maybe it was just the cooling twilight breeze.

Jocelyn had always forgiven Philip's tardiness on those Friday nights. Camping was her delight, not his. In their early years together, she hadn't insisted on much for herself. Philip had been such a refuge for her, the first solace she had known from the tempest of her family. She had been grateful to him for taking her away from that turbulence, so grateful that she went along with whatever he wanted most of the time. But when it came to the campsite and her trailer, Jocelyn held her ground. This was something she wanted for herself, something she truly enjoyed.

Rural park camping held little interest for Philip. His idea of roughing it was a hotel suite with one king-sized bed instead of two. Nonetheless, he went along with what she wanted where the camper was concerned. After a while he even seemed to enjoy the place despite himself. This evening she would have enjoyed Philip's halfhearted company, especially now that it was campfire time.

Philip had always been the one to build the campfires. That meant they wouldn't happen till late at night, when he finally arrived from downstate, or not at all on the nights he didn't make it till after Jocelyn was asleep. Jocelyn had never doubted she could manage the task herself. Several times, when she was especially exasperated that Philip couldn't manage to get here earlier, she had almost gone ahead and started the fire herself. Then she would stop herself.

Fire-building was Philip's single concession to outdoor life, his only true participation in their weekends here in Lewis County. He would carefully arrange the firewood she bought at the campground store. He would fuss with the kindling and twisted newspaper he used to start the flames, allowing her to maintain the pretense that he didn't mind these retreats to the woods that were so important to her. That way, she could quiet the guilt she had felt all her life whenever she asked anyone for anything.

Still, she had wondered why he went along with these weekends at all. Philip was not the kind of man who made concessions. He was in charge in every area of their life, and for the most part that had been all right with Jocelyn. Only on this one subject had she insisted she must have her way. She had also insisted on buying the camp trailer herself, with the money she had inherited when her grandmother died. Jocelyn had even paid for the extras—the dishes and cookware that matched the blue-and-burgundy interior, an assortment of pillows for the double bed. Philip grumbled about the foolishness of spending good money on plates and glasses when most people got by with paper and plastic. Still, he hadn't tried to stop her as she would have expected him to do.

In fact, standing up to him about these camping weekends had taught her something very valuable about Philip and their relationship. If she put her foot down, he respected her demands. At least, he had done so in this case. She hadn't done much foot-planting in their five years together. In the early years she had preferred to let him take on the burden of decision-making. She had welcomed the sense of certainty that life with a man like Philip Wald could bring. Nonetheless, that protectiveness had begun to weigh and chafe, like a yoke around her neck, several months before her final weekend here last season.

Jocelyn twisted the double thickness of pages from the *Syracuse Post Standard* sports section into a tight, long torch shape, just as Philip used to do, though he would have preferred to sacrifice the life-style section. She dropped the twist behind several others next to the rusted metal circle identical to the one on each of the eighty-five campsites here at Tranquility. She walked quickly toward the trailer, then turned back to circle the fire ring in agitated pacing steps.

Luckily, there were trees to block her campsite from its neighbors. She wouldn't want anybody to see how upset she had become all of a sudden. Like the Delaneys, her fellow campers would most likely understand, of course. Still, her guilt about her feelings for Philip, or lack of them, toward the end of his life was a subject too sensitive to share. She had never made real friends of the other campers, anyway. Philip preferred that they keep to themselves here. Jocelyn had reluctantly agreed, a concession to match his of coming here in the first place.

Jocelyn wondered if she would form any friendships this season, or even if she would come back here after this first trial weekend. Would the memories be too much for her to bear? If the unease she was feeling at this moment was an indication of what lay ahead, this visit might very well be her last to the north country. Syracuse wasn't an easy place to be, either, but there at least she wasn't so constantly reminded of why and how her husband had died and her share of the responsibility for those circumstances.

No one would question her decision should she give up the site and sell the trailer. After all, people would say, wasn't her husband on his way up here from the city the night he'd had the accident? If they had known Philip and Jocelyn better, they might even add a comment about the fact that he was only coming at all because she insisted on it. Certainly, she must have been the reason he was in such a hurry that he felt he had to fly that small plane in stormy weather. Some might even surmise the guilt she carried as a result. No one would question her decision to escape those memories.

Right now, however, she was here, and she intended to make the most of the visit, whatever her eventual decision might be. Jocelyn touched a match to the twisted paper beneath the firewood she had carefully arranged in a tepee shape. She lit several sections of the paper and watched the flames follow a crinkling brown trail toward the pile of twigs and kindling below and the logs above. Small bursts of orange and gold crackled to life as each twig ignited. Jocelyn heard the sizzle and pop of fire meeting damp places in the bark as the first log began to burn. Carefully she prodded it with a branch that was too green to catch fire easily. The floor of the fire ring glowed a deep shimmering magenta, and heat rose in waves to warm her cheeks.

Jocelyn smiled to herself. This would be a good fire. She could tell that from this strong start. Patient attention would be needed, but before long she would be watching a dance of flame, licking and pooling and sending up showers of red-orange pinpricks of light.

A bullfrog thrummed his night call from a marsh bottom on the other side of the woods. Jocelyn lifted her head to listen and to breathe in the soft sweetness of the night air, along with the more pungent scent of charring wood. The fire was already high enough to cast a play of moving light and shadow on the wide trunks and full foliage that bordered the campsite. Her glance had passed the shape that shouldn't be there before she realized what she had seen.

Somebody was standing just behind the closest line of trees. The light was only intermittent in that spot, so she couldn't be certain what the person was doing. Still, a chill crept along her flesh. She sensed that the stranger was watching her as intently as she had been staring into the fire only a moment ago.

Then, in the next flicker of flame glow, the figure was gone. Jocelyn was sure this was no trick of vision. Someone had been watching her. A memory of that afternoon and the angry woman about to collide with the car caused Jocelyn to shiver. Could this be the same woman? The figure had been clad in denim, so there was no telling the gender.

Or could she have been deluded by the firelight, after all? Could this be just another of the unsettling feelings she'd been experiencing at the Genessee Street house, as well? She had felt as if she was being watched there also, as if a presence of some kind was in the house with her or sneaking furtive glances through the windows. Of course, there was no proof that anyone was actually spying on her. In fact, there was evidence to the contrary.

Nonetheless, an instinct as old as the night told her she hadn't imagined the person in the trees just now. That same instinct cautioned her that this person, whoever it might be, could mean her harm. Jocelyn didn't take the time to ponder what the specific nature of that harm might be. She turned and hurried to the trailer, then locked herself inside.

She had left a single light burning near the double sliding doors that led from the deck she'd had built the year before. Those doors and their wide vista of the outdoors had been a major attraction for Jocelyn when she picked out this trailer. Now they made her feel exposed and vulnerable. She pulled the drapes across the opening and snapped the blinds shut over the window in the opposite wall. So many windows! She hurried into the bedroom, turning on lights along the way.

She had made this room especially homey, with her favorite books filling the stand beside the comfortable double bed and a soft reading lamp on the table. A thick, blue tufted carpet was deliberately color coordinated with the summer quilt, and the bed was topped with all those pillows she had bought for nestling into. Jocelyn had enjoyed many a contented evening snuggled up in this cheerful little room, enjoying a good story and a mug of Ovaltine while the scent of the summer night wafted through the windows.

Some of Jocelyn's most relaxed country moments had been spent either in this bedroom or at the round table on the deck beneath the colorfully striped sun umbrella. She had found true peace in these places, but there was no peace for her here tonight. What had once been cozy now felt cramped and without possibility of refuge.

Jocelyn hurried back into the living room and kitchen area to turn on more lights. She even lit the fluorescent bulb in the small bathroom. She could imagine how brightly this trailer must appear to be aglow from the outside, but that was exactly what she wanted. No one would be likely to bother her or come lurking around such a well-lit place. In fact, she would turn on the outside lights, as well. That would definitely discourage intruders. Jocelyn was about to flip that switch, which was next to the sliding glass doors, when she peeked out for a moment through the opening in the drapes. What she saw made her stop short and reconsider.

The fire she had been so proud of had guttered down into the grate beyond the deck. All that remained visible were occasional sparks dancing above the metal wall of the protective ring. Jocelyn had looked forward to building that fire into a warm blaze and maybe even toasting some marshmallows over it. She had anticipated dragging her lawn chair into the circle of warmth and spending a quiet hour there, doing nothing more taxing than feeding and prodding the flames. She had hoped to recapture some of what she remembered so fondly from summers past. Instead, she was cowering behind the curtains, too scared to venture more than a furtive glance outside.

Jocelyn had experienced this same kind of panicky moment several times since Philip's death, and more often lately. She would be in the house, usually at night. She would suddenly feel that presence watching her. At the same moment, she would be reminded that she was a woman virtually alone in the world and certainly alone at that moment. Her stomach would twist tight while her throat did the same and her mouth went dry. For several seconds, she would dart through her memory banks for someone to call, someplace to run. Then, she would force herself to calm down, pulling in deep breaths and easing them out slowly till the moment passed. She would urge herself to continue whatever she had been doing when the feeling struck, telling herself that this was her life now and she had to maintain her control over it, though not much control was necessary.

Her husband had been a methodical man who paid attention to detail. The finances were up-to-date and in the hands of a competent accountant. All Jocelyn had to do was pick up the phone if she needed funds or wanted to check if some bill or other had been taken care of. Philip had arranged for a handyman to take care of the house and a yard man to take care of the yard. The mechanic at their regular garage knew everything there was to know about the Wald cars and would even tell her when they needed to be traded in.

Philip had taken care of everything to the extent that even with him no longer physically around, he was still an influence on the day-to-day course of her life, making certain all ran smoothly just as he had always done—just as she had always been more than willing to let him do. Jocelyn had wondered if that could be the source of the presence she kept feeling. Perhaps she was only reacting to the continuing structure that Philip had created and then left behind.

While Philip was alive, Jocelyn had found that structure comforting—a haven of control after the anxiety of growing up with her flaky mother at the helm of their constantly floundering family ship. For several months after Philip's death, Jocelyn had enjoyed the lull of security that her regulated life provided. It shielded her somewhat from the grief and guilt she couldn't help feeling.

Then, a few weeks ago, she had begun to grow restless, as if the rebirth of spring had germinated fresh shoots of vitality in her as well as in the ground. Gradually, she had come to recognize that the machine of her existence was not only a convenience, it was a trap—with her caught inside. There might be nothing diabolical about the mechanistic wheels that ran her life, but there was something deadening about allowing their steady grind to remain in charge.

One of the purposes of coming here this weekend, or for however long she decided to stay, was to get herself out of Philip's well-ordered world for a while and see how well she could manage. She had told herself that she wanted to be the one taking the responsibility and the risks for a change. Yet here she was, cringing behind the draperies, needing the reassurance of every electric light in the place just to spend a single night out from under the protective mantle that was Philip's legacy.

After all, that person in the trees might have been there for a perfectly innocent reason, like gazing up at the stars or waiting for the dog to relieve himself or even out of curiosity. So what if someone had been watching her. Couldn't she handle that? Wouldn't she have to learn to handle it if she couldn't now?

Jocelyn told herself to ignore the intuition that there was something more sinister than idle curiosity about the figure in the trees. The restlessness that brought her here was partly the result of her sensing a watchful presence in the Genessee Street house with her. She wouldn't let herself think about that, either. Still, there was nothing wrong with being cautious. Jocelyn grabbed a butcher knife from the kitchen drawer. She filled her arms with more scrap newsprint for rekindling the fire and took a deep breath before stepping outside.

The scent of the night was dark and slightly damp after the humidity of the day. She could almost smell things growing in the moist earth and hear the leaves waving their green essence into the breeze. There was the pungency of campfires, as well, what remained of hers and also others, probably still crackling brightly beyond the trees. Jocelyn had pulled on a sweatshirt earlier, so she was prepared for the coolness of the evening and welcomed its refreshing brush against her cheek. She was glad she had decided to come outside again and stole only a brief glance toward the place where her surprise visitor had stood in the foliage.

She had brought a flashlight with her and used it to oversee the rebuilding of the campfire. She allowed herself only a small tug of apprehension when she snapped the flashlight off and was left with just the flickering flames to illuminate the deepening darkness. After prodding the logs into an impressive glow, she pulled the lounge chair into the circle of the fire and sat down. Snatches of music drifted in from beyond the trees where someone was enjoying their tape deck or CD player. Jocelyn didn't recognize the tune, but she hummed along, anyway, and rocked gently to the soothing rhythm.

Jocelyn had chosen this particular site specifically for its isolation. She even paid extra for leasing what would ordinarily have been space enough for two trailers, just so she could be out of sight of her neighbors. Relaxing here now, she was grateful for that privacy, but also for the strains of melody that assured her there were other people nearby. Still, those people were far enough away that the sound of them was background rather than intrusion. Over the man-made music, she could still hear the music of the night. Jocelyn was thinking how comforting that natural music could be when she heard something that was not comforting at all.

She told herself that twigs snapped and foliage rustled in the outdoors all the time. There were small animals in this part of the country, and she was no greenhorn city slicker who panicked at the sight of a raccoon or even a skunk. Then she heard more snapping and rustling, and it was precisely because she wasn't a city slicker that she sat up straight in her lawn chair and listened intently.

Whatever was moving through the woods right now was considerably larger than a raccoon, and it was definitely headed in her direction.

Jocelyn's first impulse was to jump up and dash back to the trailer, but she had done that once already this evening. She was determined not to do it again. Instead, she felt around in the grass next to the chair where she had dropped the butcher knife. Her fingers touched the hardwood handle and gripped it tight, but she didn't raise it where it would be visible in the firelight. Jocelyn stiffened her backbone and assured herself that she was ready for whatever might occur. She was also aware that she hadn't taken a full, relaxed breath since she heard the first crackle in the underbrush. And now there was much more crackling, ever closer at hand.

Chapter Two

He was definitely not a raccoon, unless those furry creatures come in a six-foot-plus model. Jocelyn was also still thinking clearly enough to doubt that this was the same person she had seen in the woods earlier. This man seemed much larger, more imposing. Of course, she only caught a fleeting glimpse of her previous visitor, and she had been on the verge of panic when she did. Maybe she shouldn't trust her recollections of that moment.

Jocelyn maintained her stranglehold on the knife handle as he entered the circle of firelight, but she kept it out of his line of vision. He moved with the lumbering grace of a big man who has come to terms with his size. He did round his shoulders slightly, quite possibly the result of having to lean forward to hear companions of more usual height. Ordinarily, Jocelyn might have been alarmed to have this mountain of an individual appear so suddenly out of the darkness, especially after her two scares today. Instead, the instinct that had told her to beware earlier now told her she had nothing to fear from this man.

She let the knife slip back to the ground near her chair. She was about to greet him, maybe even to stand up as she did so, when he reached the area of firelight bright enough to make his face truly visible to her for the first time. What she saw there kept her rooted in her seat, the intended words unspoken in her throat.

His features were on the square side but not unpleasantly so. His face suited the rugged angles of the rest of him. His forehead was high and wide and clear of so much as a wrinkle or worry line. His eyes were hooded by prominent eyebrow ridges, but she guessed they were smiling by the crinkling at the corners. They were also looking steadily and directly at her. She couldn't help but wonder what he saw.

"You're Jocelyn Wald," he said. "We've never met, but I've known who you are for a long time. I'm Clint Conti."

His hand reached out to shake hers. She pondered why and how he knew who she was when she couldn't recall ever having seen him before. His hand was wide and square. She would have preferred to ignore its presence. Having her fingers engulfed by his great paw wasn't what she wanted right now. But she was in the country, where they set considerable store by courtesy. She had better not be rude.

Because he was so tall, she would have to get out of her lounge chair to reach him. She was about to do that when he stepped forward, stooped toward her and took hold of her left elbow. In less than a breath of time, she was on her feet, lifted there as effortlessly as if she had been a feather cushion. He released her arm as quickly as he had taken it and stepped away from her again, seemingly aware how overwhelming it could become to have somebody his size towering over her.

He didn't offer the handshake again, and Jocelyn felt suddenly awkward to be standing in front of him this way in the firelight. Since his back was to the flames, she could no longer see his eyes clearly enough to tell where he was looking. That made her more awkward still. She had thought of herself as a married woman for years now, even in the months since Philip's death. As such, she had not considered herself the object of interest to men other than her husband. That interest might have been there among the men she encountered, but since it was of no importance to her she simply didn't see it. She was hardly so oblivious right now.

Jocelyn could actually, physically feel his gaze traveling over her, down her body and back up again, pausing for an intense moment at the mound of her breasts beneath her bulky sweatshirt and the tight pull of denim across her thighs. She gave herself a small shake to clear her head, and other parts, of this ridiculous fantasy. The tense moments of this generally overwrought day must have affected her more deeply than she realized.

"I'm pleased to meet you, Mr. Conti," she said, snapping herself out of whatever wild digression had just afflicted her. "Are you camping here? I don't believe we've met before."

"The Delaneys are friends of mine. I help them out sometimes. But, no, I'm not a camper. I'm what they call a local."

"You mean you live around here."

"That's right."

He turned toward the fire and picked up her green branch from the ground. He nudged one log off another, and a gust of flame and sparks erupted between. He stood with the fingers of one hand slipped inside the pocket of his close-fitting jeans and his weight shifted toward that side. He concentrated on the fire, staring into its depths as Jocelyn had been doing a few moments before. She could see his features clearly now, including his eyes. Their expression of rapt attention was more contemplative than brooding. Had he said he did odd jobs for the Delaneys? He certainly didn't look like a handyman, despite a physique that would make him equal to just about any physical task.

"Do you work around here, too?" she asked, realizing how inane that must sound. After all, if he lived in the area, he must also work in the area. Jocelyn was curious enough about him to risk coming across as a bit foolish.

He turned to look at her with a wry smile, as if he might have figured out that she was fishing for details. "Not really. I ran a contracting business in Albany. I might do something like that here. For now, I'm just getting used to being back in the north country."

"I see." So she'd been right. He wasn't a handyman, at least not by profession.

"What about you?"

He'd stopped prodding the fire, and focused his attention on her. She could see where his gaze was directed now. He was looking into her face. The earlier sensation had returned, as if he were brushing her body with his eyes.

"What about me?" There she went, sounding inane again.

"I know you don't live in the immediate vicinity. You're from Syracuse, aren't you?"

"Yes, I am." Jocelyn sat back down in the lawn chair. She would have an easier time maintaining her composure from a seated position. "But I'm not employed there. I...well, my husband."

"I know about your husband. I'm sorry."

He said it softly and with caring in his voice. He didn't make her feel pitiable the way other people sometimes did. Instead, it occurred to Jocelyn that she could probably talk to him about what had been going on with her since Philip's death. This Clint Conti person would not only listen but understand, maybe even have some insight that would help her understand better herself.

More foolishness on her part, imagining that a perfect stranger could be confidant to her most intimate thoughts. Maybe she was a lot more emotionally needy than she had realized. Maybe she was pitiable, after all.

Jocelyn murmured a thank-you for his condolences. "This is the first time I've been back here since it happened."

"Yes, I know."

Jocelyn looked sharply at him. "How do you know that?"

Now it was his turn to feel awkward. She could tell that by the way he shifted his weight forward and then back again in a halting movement very unlike the smooth, ambling gait with which he'd walked over here. He resumed his poking at the fire, more forcefully this time. Flames shot upward, like the exhalation of a fiery beast lurking among the magenta coals.

"I'd have noticed if you were here, just like I noticed you last summer."

He looked over at her. The long stick remained where he had thrust it into the fire. Jocelyn avoided his eyes by staring at the stick and wondering how long it would take to be set ablaze.

"Does your family live around here, too?" she asked. His eyes weren't the only thing she intended to avoid. She didn't care to acknowledge his last comment, either.

"My parents are in Lowville now. They used to own a farm about twenty miles from here, but they've retired from farming. My sister and her family moved down near Boonville. I've got assorted aunts, uncles and cousins scattered around the county, too."

"It must feel good to be nearby so much family."

"These days it feels good. When I was younger, I felt surrounded."

"But you stuck around, anyway." Jocelyn knew she was being inquisitive, maybe too much so. But she was curious about him.

"Actually, I didn't." He was staring into the fire again and poking it occasionally. The stick hadn't caught fire yet. "I went off to see the world, and let it see me."

"But you came back here again."

"Yes, I did. I . . ." He paused to look over at her again.

He had an odd, questioning look in his eyes. She wondered if he felt the same thing she did, the intimacy of the small circle of firelight and warmth, as if they could share all their secrets in hushed, private tones and never fear betrayal.

"I have a house here," he said after a moment's contemplation. Somehow, she sensed it wasn't what he had been about to say before. "I built it over several summers. It's back in the woods not too far from here. I decided to find out what it would be like to live there for a while."

"I see."

Jocelyn suspected there was more to be learned, between the lines of his story. But she had felt him move away from the intimacy of the firelight circle, at least emotionally. She had always been able to do that with people, get inside what they were feeling. It was a skill she'd picked up from living with her mother, when survival had often depended on figuring out how far off the planet Mama was flying that day. In this case, that particular talent of Jocelyn's told her Mr. Conti had satisfied her curiosity about him as much as he intended to at the moment.

As a further signal of that, he gave the topmost log one last prod, then dropped the stick on the ground and stepped away to the other side of the fire. He was turned partly away from her, so she could see the angle of his cheekbone and the height of his forehead. He leaned back to gaze up at the stars. He flexed his shoulders, and she could see the muscles shift beneath his faded denim jacket.

The rosy glow of the firelight danced along what she could make out of his features, first illuminating his resolute chin, then the hollow beneath the cheekbones, then the ridge of brow above his deep-set eyes. She examined each element of his face as it moved in and out of sight like a flickering lantern slide. She wouldn't have wanted him to know she was studying him so closely. For the time being his attention was concentrated elsewhere, not on her.

He stood transfixed, as if absorbed in the vista above them. He might have forgotten she was there altogether. Jocelyn followed his gaze heavenward, to the mass of stars that always struck her as startling in number on a clear night like this. She felt the stillness of the night and knew he must be feeling it too. He exhaled an extended sigh. Again he breathed in deeply. She did the same.

When he spoke, he did so in a voice that was pitched low but still audible. "This is good," he said.

Jocelyn's own voice caught in her throat, and she had to keep herself from gasping aloud as his words struck a note of resonance in her that she hadn't known was there. In that instant, the stars grew even brighter against the darkened sky.

She whispered in reply, "Yes, it is."

They stayed like that a while longer, silently sharing a moment beyond words. Then he turned back toward her with a slow smile, like a traveler in reverie reluctantly returning to the real world.

"It's getting late," he said. "I'd better be going."

Jocelyn resisted the urge to invite him to stay and stare at the stars with her a little longer. "Yes, it's getting late," she said.

He was looking at her intently again. She could tell that by the way his brows had knitted together. "Are you all right here by yourself?" he asked.

That was a question Philip had asked her often, as if she were too helpless to take care of herself for a few hours outside the immediate circle of his protection. She had come to resent the inference more and more in the months before his death, and she didn't much appreciate it now.

"Of course I'm all right," she said. "Why wouldn't I be?"

He continued studying her for a moment. One eyebrow had arched briefly in reaction to the sudden sharpness of her tone.

"Right," he said. "Why wouldn't you be?"

He shifted himself to a more alert posture, and Jocelyn could tell he was about to leave. She thought he might offer her another handshake. She was ready to respond with a firm grip that would assure him of her self-sufficiency. Instead, he only nodded and smiled.

"Sleep well," he said, stepping backward toward the edge of the firelight. He was still facing her as he paused. "I'll see you again."

Even without the resolute set of his chin, Jocelyn would have known that was true. She would see him again. She wondered whether she wanted to. Before she could come up with an answer or even return his goodbye, he was striding away and she was alone once more by the campfire.

Jocelyn woke up early the next morning. She did that in the country. The clamor of bird calls always sounded as if they were determined to outdo the frog chorus of the night before in the decibel department. No alarm clock was necessary, but she didn't mind. Weather permitting, her first coffee of the day would be enjoyed on the deck before the sun had dried the dew from the grass.

She stretched long beneath the light comforter. The cool breeze through the slatted window was finishing the wake-up job the birds had begun. Jocelyn tossed aside the covers and swung her legs over the side of the bed. She'd worn an oversized T-shirt to bed, and so merely had to pull on a pair of black leggings and slip her feet into yellow plastic thongs to be dressed. She would add her ancient denim jacket just before going outside. She might not be able to get away with such a casual outfit in the city, but here it was perfect for early morning under the sun umbrella.

A few moments later, the kitchen area was fragrant with rich coffee aroma. Jocelyn filled her favorite mug, the black one with the trail of gilt-trimmed Egyptian cats around the sides. She'd make herself her daily oatmeal later on, but right now she had to get outdoors before the dewy time was gone for today.

She was pushing the sliding doors open when she noticed the butcher knife where she had dropped it last night, on top of the cabinet next to the built-in tape deck and radio. She touched the handle and ran her fingers along the cool metal of the blade. The sharpness sent fear coursing through her, the same fear she had felt last night.

She had been in danger. Someone had been lurking in the woods, watching her. Jocelyn's sensible instincts told her this was true. That person had not been a dog walker or a casual stroller, no matter how much she preferred to think it. That person had been spying on her, as if she were a specimen on a glass slide with no more right to privacy or respect than a bit of protoplasm.

Jocelyn slammed the knife down on the counter and hurried out to the deck. Last night would not have happened when Philip was alive. For these past ten months she had been a woman alone in a threatening world. Last night that threat had become a reality. This time, she had faced the situation down and conquered her fear. She wondered if she would be able to do that again. She wondered if she was equal to the demands of this new world she had so newly entered.

Yet, she had felt something else besides fear last night. She remembered it now. She would have to call it exhilaration. She had been totally alert, with every sense tuned to its utmost pitch and ready to respond at an instant's notice. She had been scared, but she had also been confident. She smiled to herself as she leaned back in her white deck chair and propped her feet up on the one across from it.

She pictured herself walking into the darkness, determined to face whatever might be out there, clutching her weapon at the ready. Philip would have thought that a ludicrous sight. He might even have laughed at her. She didn't care about that. She was proud of the feisty woman she'd been last night. She suspected that woman would be inside her when she was needed.

There was one more thing, also. She had met a man she found attractive. The surge of confidence she had been enjoying just a moment ago waned at the thought. She could see Clint Conti's handsome profile as he gazed up at the stars. She could feel the tension that had whipped her insides into turmoil at the sight of his powerful body silhouetted against the firelight. The sound of his voice, echoing a promise of depth and strength, ran along her nerve endings once more.

Jocelyn put her hand to her throat, as if to touch the breath that had caught there. This was a challenge she felt less equal to. She would almost rather charge into the darkness to confront a mad prowler than face the threat of a man like Clint and what he had awakened in her, if only for a moment, last night. That part of her had been slumbering all of her life. She knew it was there. She also knew that it was untested, as she was. She did not know what it would be like to find herself in the grips of the force called passion. She had experienced a taste of that last night. For that moment, she had been as out of control as she had ever been under Philip's dominance, maybe more so. She didn't think she liked that. Yet, part of her longed to feel it again.

Dangerous territory, Jocelyn warned herself. She had no idea who Clint Conti was or what his intentions to-

might be. He could very well be the lurking
....er. Last night, she had thought Clint must be
.igger and taller than the figure she had seen among
the trees. This morning, she wasn't so sure. She could
have been deceived by the confusing messages her body
was sending. Maybe she didn't think Clint was the
prowler because she didn't want him to be. Maybe
there was more to fear from him than the power of his
sexuality.

She tried to hear what her instincts were telling her.
She had always possessed an ability to read people. She
had developed that talent as a defensive strategy during her childhood. She could usually read herself, as
well. She could train that vision inside and instruct
herself to be totally honest about what she was truly
feeling. She concentrated on doing that now, but all
that came through was more confusion.

Jocelyn was surprised. No matter how uncertain and
unsettling life with her mother had been, Jocelyn had
always kept herself on top of things. Even before pu-
berty, she had trained herself to function as an adult,
but she had long resented the circumstances requiring
her to be mature beyond her chronological age. Now,
for the first time, she recognized another side of those
years. She had felt confident back then, like last night,
and fully alive, too, in a way the insulated comfort of
her life with Philip had caused her to forget. She had
felt in control; and she had liked that, whether she realized it at the time or not.

Jocelyn slapped her feet down on the deck. She
grabbed her mug from the table and charged to the
trailer door. She wasn't about to step back under anybody's control, especially not a man's. She was her
own woman now, and she was going to stay that way.

She slid the screen door open and stepped inside. In the kitchen area she turned the sink tap on a bit too hard to rinse her mug, and water splashed the front of her T-shirt. She had already resolved, before coming up here this weekend, that she wasn't going to hide from life any longer and she wasn't going to run away from anything, either.

The concept of running away froze her where she stood for a moment, with her hand still on the tap and water still running in the sink. An image flashed across her thoughts, as real as if it had been happening this very instant. She saw herself clutching the wheel of the Lincoln and tromping down on the accelerator so hard that the big car skidded onto the soft shoulder and nearly fishtailed off the road. In the rearview mirror she could see the woman running after her, wild hair flying, her face contorted from shouting epithets Jocelyn could no longer hear because she was too intent upon running away.

She had behaved just as Philip would have expected her to do. Jocelyn turned off the tap and set the mug upside down in the blue dish-drainer basket. She had resolved to stand firm and face whatever confronted her. Then, she had violated that resolve. She wiped her hands resolutely on a blue plaid dish towel. Now, she would have to correct that error.

JOCELYN DROVE along the road back toward the vegetable stand at a more cautious speed than she had left it yesterday afternoon. The map told her that this area was called Tug Hill, a vast plateau that rose from the edge of Lake Ontario miles away. Winters were legendary here, with snow piling many feet deep at some points and making these old, neglected roads all but impassable. There had been attempts to settle the plateau and make it productive. In the end, the rugged landscape and harsh weather defeated those settlers. Some said they called the place Tug Hill because it had tugged the heart out of so many good farmers. Only the native people had survived the rigors of this part of the country for long. According to Iroquois myth, their people had literally sprung forth from the ground here.

The Iroquois were gone now, along with just about everyone else. All that remained were a few families living mostly on dilapidated farms far distant from one another. Otherwise, there were only relics, ghostly reminders such as the fallen-down house Jocelyn had just passed. Grayed spokes were silhouetted against the sky where the roof had caved in, and the lower floor was obscured by foliage gone wild. Two fields farther along the road, she saw the stone slabs of an overgrown graveyard. Many of the stones had been knocked off kilter by the upheavals of nature and maybe a vandal or two.

Those forgotten tombstones struck a chill through Jocelyn and raised goose flesh on her arms, though the morning was warm and getting warmer. She remembered hearing one of the locals remark once that this was God's country and God wanted to keep it to himself so he had driven everybody away. That might explain why she felt like such an intruder here this morning, as if she had strayed off the civilized map and was on her own where legend still claimed the occasional panther sighting. Even the high, deep blue of the sky and the prevalence of birdsong could not dispel the desolation of such a wild, abandoned countryside.

Jocelyn thought about turning the Lincoln around and driving straight out of here the way she came.

Something told her this would be the wise course to take, but she wasn't about to give in to panic. She tingled with apprehension nonetheless.

Her pulse tripped faster than usual. Her breath was shallow and high in her throat. She suspected that if she stopped to listen she would be able to hear the beating of her heart and the singing of blood through her veins. She had no intention of stopping until she had confronted yesterday's fear without Philip or anyone else to stand up to it for her. Around the next bend in the road she recognized the opportunity to do just that.

Chapter Three

At first Jocelyn thought the vegetable stand was deserted. She pulled the car to a stop, anyway, and got out. Then she saw a man. He was slouched in a kitchen chair tilted back against the weathered rear wall of the lean-to. The two rear chair legs dug into the ground several inches up their tubular chrome length. The vinyl of the backrest was split, and the seat was partway detached from the frame. Jocelyn guessed that those inches of earth might be all that kept the chair from collapsing altogether and toppling its occupant to the ground.

"What can I do you for?" he asked.

For a moment she was at a loss for an answer. What *was* she doing here?

"I'm looking for somebody I saw here yesterday."

"Are you really, now?"

He did turn around as he said that. She had already noted that his hair was long and unevenly cut. He wore a dark, faded T-shirt and a vest that had once belonged to a suit but was now decades out of style and split at the armpits by the considerable expanse of his shoulders and biceps. His face was tanned more gray than brown and covered by stubble on the lower half.

His eyes were slitted too narrowly to make their color visible, and he was grinning at her in a way she found much too familiar for comfort. Still, she stood her ground.

"There was a young woman here yesterday afternoon. She had long dark hair."

"Like mine?" he grinned and fingered a scraggly lock just below his ears.

Jocelyn swallowed her uneasiness. "I didn't get a very good look at her."

"As a matter of fact, she had hair just like mine," he said, drawling out the words as if to prolong the suspense he seemed to know they were creating. "As a matter of fact, all us Mapeses got the same color hair and the same eyes, too. But DeDe's got the worst temper. I expect you already know that."

"Is that her name? DeDe?" Jocelyn waited a moment for an answer, but he just kept grinning at her. "Would you know what her reason might have been for chasing after me yesterday even though I've never laid eyes on her before?"

"I expect it was more that big boat of yours she was chasing after." He nodded toward the Lincoln.

"Why would she do that?"

"Maybe she thought it was hers. Maybe she thought you took it from her. Don't you know, all us Mapeses got big old lux-u-ry cars like that one."

His mocking sneer was grating on Jocelyn's nerves. She'd run into this north country roundaboutness before, though never in such a surly tone. Still, she'd had the feeling on occasion in the past that she was being made to earn whatever information she was after by enduring a disquisition like this one, full of meandering, maddening circles around the subject before zeroing in. She had learned from those experiences that impatience on her part would only defeat her purpose. She forced herself to keep that lesson in mind now.

"Is DeDe available for me to speak to?"

He laughed. "Available? She wouldn't care much to hear you call her that. My sister likes to think of herself as the hard-to-get type. Except in some special cases, that is."

He nodded toward the Lincoln again, and suddenly his grin was gone. Jocelyn sensed menace as palpable as the graveled ground beneath her feet. Common sense pleaded for her to get back in her car and drive away. She was tempted, but she didn't.

"Is your sister here?"

"She's up at the house," he said in a flat tone of voice. Apparently, he had lost interest in mocking Jocelyn.

"Will you take me to her?"

"I'm supposed to stay down here till noon."

"Maybe you could leave for just a few minutes." She looked around, from the few bedraggled vegetables on the front shelf of the lean-to to the deserted road beyond her parked car.

"You got that right," he said, following her gaze. "We don't do too much business out this way."

"Then why do you keep this stand here?" Her curiosity wouldn't let her resist asking that.

He stared at her for a moment, as if she had said something that made no sense at all. "Because we always have." He hoisted himself out of the chair. "Come on. I'll take you up to the house."

He wasn't particularly tall, but he made up in muscular breadth what he lacked in height. Jocelyn guessed he would be a formidable opponent in any physical

confrontation. He had already begun to walk toward
a path that was barely discernible amid the underbrush beyond the stand. Suddenly, she wasn't so certain she should be following this guy into the
wilderness. How did she know he wasn't lying to her?
Maybe he didn't really have a sister. Maybe he was
luring Jocelyn into the woods to do her harm.

"Are you coming or what?"

He was at the edge of the graveled clearing that
served as parking area for the vegetable stand. He had
paused to look back at her. He didn't appear particularly menacing. He wasn't even sneering any longer. If
his attention had been captured by her a few moments
ago, she had obviously since passed the limits of its
span.

"Suit yourself," he said. "I'm going to get myself a
cola. You can come along or not."

He headed onto the path and into the trees at an angle away from the road. His pace was ambling but deliberate, as if he really did have his own destination in
mind and couldn't care less whether she accompanied
him. Jocelyn took a deep breath and reminded herself
that she had decided to take some risks in this new
phase of life she was embarking upon. Still, she wished
she had that butcher knife from last night to tip the
odds a bit more in her favor. She followed Mapes onto
the path all the same, but kept enough distance away
to allow herself a running start if needed.

The trees were thick here—maples, elms, birch,
poplars. Jocelyn strained to see ahead through them,
but the profusion of early summer leaves kept her in
suspense until the clearing burst upon them near the
top of the rise. She had expected more weathered siding, like that up the road. So many Tug Hill houses had

been worn to smooth silvery boards by the unyielding environment. They might never have known the slap of a paintbrush for all you could tell by looking at them now. Jocelyn assumed the Mapes place would be something on that order. She was wrong.

The house was a wood frame and not overlarge, two stories with a porch across the front. It had been painted white, obviously quite regularly, and planters brimming with red and pink impatiens hung by lengths of varicolored macramé above the porch rail. More blooms bordered the porch steps in well-tended beds. Along the edges of the clearing, before it gave way to trees again at the side and back of the house, wildflowers grew in lovely clusters. Forget-me-nots, white anemones, purple columbine, daisies and black-eyed Susans sprouted from grass so free from weeds that there had to have been a taming human hand at work among them.

The screen door at the back of the porch squeaked on the hinges as it opened. Jocelyn was surprised that whoever was in charge of this much-cared-for place had let even that small squeak go uncorrected. The young woman who stood in the doorway looked as if she might very well be that person. She regarded Jocelyn with a level gaze and not a trace of wildness in her eyes. DeDe Mapes's dark brown hair was pulled back at the nape of her neck instead of flying about her face the way it had yesterday as she ran after Jocelyn's car. If DeDe did have the worst temper in the Mapes family, as her brother claimed, there was none of it visible today.

"Do you like flowers?" asked DeDe, probably because she had been watching from behind the dark screen as Jocelyn looked the place over. "Reggie never mentioned that about you."

Jocelyn had reached the foot of the porch steps. She stopped there. Brother Mapes had mounted to the porch ahead of her and moved off to the side where he lounged against the railing and watched.

"I don't believe I know anybody named Reggie," Jocelyn said.

"You knew him, all right," Brother Mapes sneered. "You just didn't know you knew him."

"Shut up, Davis." DeDe didn't look at her brother when she said that, but he shrugged his acquiescence all the same.

DeDe stepped forward to the edge of the porch. The breeze rippled her long, full skirt. She had on white canvas flats and a sleeveless top that matched the soft turquoise of some of the large swirls in the skirt pattern. Her arms were tanned a pleasant shade of brown. Her features were strong but regular, and she was quite attractive.

"You'd better come up here and sit down," she said to Jocelyn. "I think you'll be needing a seat when you hear what I have to say."

Jocelyn hesitated. She didn't really trust DeDe's calm exterior. She might not be running and gesturing like a madwoman as she had been yesterday, but there was something other than calmness beneath her surface. Jocelyn could feel a controlled tension.

"Come on up here," the brother urged. "DeDe won't bite you. That ain't her style, at least not till she gives you fair warning."

"Davis, I told you to stay out of this. Now get back on down to the stand where you belong."

Davis wasn't much taller than DeDe, but he was certainly more powerfully built. Nonetheless, he shrugged again and pulled himself up from the rail.

"That's right. I sure wouldn't want to miss out on all the vegetable business we're going to do today" was all he said as he clumped down the porch steps, then off along the path to the woods. Apparently, he'd forgotten about being thirsty for a cola.

"Don't mind him," DeDe said. "My brothers just need somebody to keep them in line now and then."

Jocelyn could see that sister DeDe was precisely the person to do that line tending.

"He's right about me not being about to bite you," DeDe went on. "You gave me a big shock yesterday. That got my dander up. Once I get a mad on like that, there's no stopping me. I don't let it happen too often. So, you can stand there while I tell you what I got to say or you can take a seat up here. It's all the same to me because I'm going to take a load off no matter what you do."

True to her word, DeDe turned away and walked off to the side of the porch where two cushioned rockers faced out toward the railing and the view of the countryside beyond. Jocelyn was still apprehensive, but she was also curious to find out what this young woman could be talking about. This could all be a case of mistaken identity, but something told Jocelyn that DeDe Mapes was usually too deliberate a person to make many mistakes. Jocelyn climbed to the porch and walked over to the empty chair, glad that DeDe had left her the one nearest the steps.

"I take care of things around here for my dad and my brothers," DeDe said, confirming what Jocelyn had already suspected. "I been doing that ever since I got out of high school. Teachers said I should go to college, but we couldn't manage that even if they got me a scholarship. So I stayed around here. Could've gotten married a couple of times, but I didn't see much future in it. Would've been the same as doing for my dad and my brothers, only with more chance of problems in the long run. Besides, I never was in love with anybody. Not till I met Reggie."

DeDe paused and gazed out across the trees. The Tug Hill plateau was not so flat that there weren't occasional hillocks such as this one to afford a picturesque view. The fields beyond the trees were green, yellow and beige. In the far distance, a sliver of the surface of Lake Ontario shone along the horizon in the sun. DeDe Mapes was staring in that direction, but Jocelyn had the feeling she wasn't seeing the landscape.

"Is that the Reggie your brother says I know? I really don't remember meeting anybody named Reggie."

DeDe's head snapped around toward Jocelyn in the first betrayal of anything other than calm she had displayed. "Look. I didn't mean for any of this to happen. It just did. Reggie should have been the one to straighten things out. He said he would, then it was too late. I almost did it myself, like I always do everything myself, but I didn't want to mess it up with him." She sighed and seemed to crumple a little. "Besides, he didn't even know I'd figured out who you were, much less that I'd figured out who he was."

A fearful tremor caught at Jocelyn's throat, a premonition she would have liked to ignore but couldn't. "I really don't know what you're talking about. What does this Reggie and all the rest of it have to do with me? Reggie who?"

DeDe was calm again as she studied Jocelyn, but the tension was even more visible now. The effort to hold herself in check had pulled the skin tight and rigid over DeDe's cheekbones and around her mouth.

"With me he was Reggie Williams," DeDe said, "but he had another name. His other name was Philip Wald."

Jocelyn's voice felt as if it had drifted off over the trees beyond her reach. She opened her mouth to protest, but nothing came out. DeDe was mistaken. There could be no question of that. Yet, the foreboding Jocelyn had experienced a few moments ago was stronger than ever. It was that sense of impending doom her words had to struggle past now, while DeDe watched and waited.

What finally came out was not the denial Jocelyn had planned. "Do you have proof?" was all she asked.

DeDe reached into a pocket among the colorful folds of her skirt. She pulled out a photograph carefully preserved by a coat of lamination. The way she handled the small Kodachrome snapshot made clear how precious it must be to her. However, to Jocelyn, this piece of plastic and the images protected within it were a source of great dread. She hesitated to take hold of it as plainly as DeDe was reluctant to give it up. Jocelyn touched the corner of the proffered photo to tip it into view, but she didn't actually grasp it in her hand.

The image was a bit blurred, as if the camera might have moved or the shot had been taken hastily. DeDe was in the foreground wearing a yellow sundress. A thick lock of her long hair was caught up in a matching yellow ribbon a few inches above her ear. She was smiling, and that smile along with the hair ribbon made her seem even younger than the midtwenties she appeared to be today. She was not looking directly into the camera and appeared to be striding toward the photographer. Beyond her stood a man, facing sideways, almost out of the frame of the picture. His figure was less defined than DeDe's, but his profile was distinct enough to be recognizable.

Jocelyn did, in fact, recognize him. The man in the photograph was her late husband, Philip Wald. She drew in a deep breath as she made out the most disturbing detail of the picture. By looking more closely, she could tell that DeDe's hand was stretched behind her and Philip's was extended to the side. Just visible at the edge of DeDe's yellow sundress skirt was a partial view of those two hands—intertwined. Jocelyn stared at the lacing of those fingers, more aghast than if she had seen Philip's ghost spring to life before her eyes.

Suddenly, DeDe was talking again, rather rapidly, as if to camouflage the silent space where Jocelyn's shock and pain were a tangible living, struggling presence between them.

"I didn't know he was married when I met him," DeDe said. "I was hanging out at the airfield over near Adams. One of my brothers picks up some work there now and then. Reggie flew in and out of that strip, and one of those times we got talking. Then we went for coffee, and one thing led to another. Pretty soon he was coming to see me Fridays as soon as he got up here. We'd spend those evenings together."

So, that was why Philip was always so late getting to the trailer on Friday nights. Jocelyn could also guess where he had really been off to when he said he was going to check on the plane or wash the car or whatever.

"Eventually, I figured out that he was married," DeDe was saying. "Why else would he have to leave before midnight on a Friday? So, one night I took Davis's truck and followed Reggie, all the way to that campground where you stay. I parked the truck out on the highway and snuck around in the trees till I spotted his car. That's a nice rig you got, by the way. I couldn't see inside, but a little while later Reggie came out and started a campfire. You were there, too. That was maybe the hardest thing had ever happened to me up till then, seeing you that night."

DeDe stopped talking and gazed out over the trees again. Jocelyn felt as if she should hate this young woman. She even longed to hate her but didn't seem able to. Instead, Jocelyn could empathize with how devastated DeDe must have been to discover that the man she cared about had a wife. Jocelyn was feeling something very much like that right now. Then something else occurred to her—an image of DeDe creeping through the woods near the campsite. Could she have been the figure Jocelyn saw spying on her from the trees? In a pair of slacks or jeans, DeDe would be about the right size. Jocelyn decided not to mention that possibility right now.

"So, you were having an affair with my husband? Is that what you're telling me?"

DeDe turned to gaze at Jocelyn. DeDe's eyes were shiny, as if there might be tears there, but she didn't let them fall. "I wouldn't have called it by those words, but you're right. That's what it really was. An affair with a married man." DeDe sighed. "I never did anything like that before, and I tried to stop it. You may not believe me, but it's true. After I followed him that night, I tried to break it off. Then he told me about the problems the two of you were having."

"What problems were those?" Jocelyn said that so coldly she even startled herself.

The shock that had overwhelmed her at DeDe's revelation had begun to evolve into anger, mixed with humiliation and a sense of betrayal. At the moment, that potent emotional cocktail was running through her veins and numbing them to ice.

"I don't know if any of this is true." For the first time, DeDe sounded unsure of herself. "After all, Reggie wasn't exactly the most honest guy—to either of us."

She'd said a mouthful that time. Jocelyn nodded. "Just tell me what he told you."

"Well, he said the two of you weren't very close, that you never had been, really. But you depended on him for just about everything, so he couldn't just walk out and leave you in the lurch. He had to make sure you were taken care of before he did that."

Jocelyn let those words sink in. There was a ring of truth to them she couldn't deny. "So, he told you he was going to leave me for you?"

"Yes, he did." To DeDe's credit, she didn't appear to be finding any pleasure in these revelations. "He was going to tell you that the weekend . . . the weekend he died."

DeDe turned away, perhaps because she was having a harder time holding back the tears now. Jocelyn's fury was almost as frigid as before, but she had to acknowledge one thing. She had never felt as profound a grief at Philip's death as she saw etched in the rigid straightness of DeDe's spine or the trembling of her shoulders.

"I was going to tell him the same thing myself that weekend. I wanted to leave him, too."

Jocelyn's pride was obviously still functioning somewhere at the periphery of her emotions. She didn't want to be thought of as the dopey little wife who had been about to be dumped by her husband in favor of a newer model.

"I'm not surprised by that," DeDe said in a subdued voice. "Everything I found out about you made me think you were pretty smart and wouldn't want to hang on to something that wasn't working anymore."

"Everything you found out about me? Were you spying on me?"

"I don't blame you for not liking that part, but you were my enemy, as far as I could see. Know thine enemy, they say. So, I checked you out as best I could. Of course, there wasn't much to find out around here, since you only came up for weekends and all. But I did find out some things. That's how I got to know Reggie's name wasn't Reggie. That was when I made a big decision, too. To this day, I don't know that it was the right thing to do, but I did it, anyway."

Jocelyn wasn't sure she wanted to hear the answer, but she went ahead and asked. "What decision was that?"

"I decided not to tell Reggie I knew he was Philip Wald. I was afraid I'd scare him off if I did that, and by that time I didn't want to even think about being without him. So, I went along. I never told his friends he wasn't Reggie Williams or anything."

Jocelyn gasped. "Other people knew him by that other name?"

"Sure. Lots of them."

Jocelyn bolted straight up out of her chair. "Don't tell me any more," she blurted. "I can't hear any more. Not right now."

DeDe stood up, as well. "There's one more thing you've got to know about. There's a house. Reggie bought it. We used to go there together. It's probably yours now."

Jocelyn stared slack-jawed at DeDe. Philip had bought a house up here? Jocelyn had wanted so much for him to do that. He said he wasn't interested in living out here in the sticks, even part-time. Suddenly, Jocelyn was absolutely certain that if she heard one more word about Philip or Reggie or whoever he had really been, she was going to do something she would regret, maybe even something violent.

"I'm sorry," Jocelyn said, "but I have to go now."

She bolted for the porch steps and hurried down them.

"Will you be back?" DeDe called from the porch.

Jocelyn couldn't answer. She didn't have an answer right now, to that question or anything else she had heard this morning. All she could do was raise her hand in a vague waving gesture as she ran toward the path without looking back.

Chapter Four

Jocelyn stood by the car, rummaging for the keys. She pawed at the hodgepodge in the bottom of her purse, ready to pour it out on the dusty ground if she didn't find what she was after soon.

"Did they hurt you?"

The voice was more tense than it had been the night before, but she recognized it, anyway. Still, she spun around in surprise to find Clint Conti towering over her.

"What are you doing here?" The thought that he might be following her was even more disturbing than his closeness.

"I was driving past and saw your car here, but you were nowhere around, so I stopped to make sure you were all right. Then you came running out of the trees like the hounds were after you. Did they do something to you up there?" Clint Conti nodded toward the hillside and the Mapes house above them.

Do something? Jocelyn wanted to shout. Yes, they did something. They blew my life out from under me. That young woman says my husband bought a house for her near here. I begged him for a house like that, and he said no. Yes, they hurt me, all right. I can't remember when anybody ever hurt me more.

Those words were in Jocelyn's throat straining to burst forth, along with the tears that welled behind her eyes. She remembered her dignity and held off the outburst, distracted from it by the strangeness of Clint's question.

"Why would the Mapes family want to do anything to hurt me?" she asked.

He seemed to consider his answer before speaking. "They can be a rough bunch. Besides, you look like you're upset."

"I'm fine," Jocelyn lied as she began rummaging in her purse again.

"Can I help you with something?" He stepped even closer.

"No, thank you," she said. She moved away from him, nearly pressing herself up against the car door. "I'm just trying to find my car keys."

He touched her shoulder and moved her aside, very gently, as if he understood exactly how fragile she was feeling at the moment. He reached through the open car window and past the steering wheel. She heard a familiar jangle as he pulled the keys back through the window. They had been in the ignition where she left them.

"Why don't I give you a lift back to the camp?" he said.

"Don't be foolish," she snapped and grabbed the keys. "My car is right here. Why would I need a ride?"

"I was thinking that you might be a little too much on edge to drive."

"I'm fine," she repeated, still lying.

She knew she was being rude, but the last thing she needed right now was a drive alone with this man who set her stomach tumbling like a roller-coaster ride. She opened the car door. She hoped the cause of her agitation wasn't obvious as she got into the car and closed the door.

"You've got something caught here," he said, opening the door she'd just slammed shut.

Jocelyn hadn't noticed that her jacket had slipped from the back of the seat where she'd thrown it earlier. One sleeve had slipped down, and she had closed the door on it. Clint retrieved the sleeve and was about to tuck it back inside the car when Jocelyn noticed that a line of black grease from the door frame had marred the beige cotton material.

Suddenly, she wanted in the worst way to burst out crying. The tears were still there behind her eyes. The sobs were strangling in her throat. She understood vaguely, somewhere at the corner of her consciousness, that those sobs weren't really about the stain on her jacket. They had to do with a dead husband who'd had a secret life, and this other man who set her nerves jangling. If she didn't get out of here she was going to make a spectacle of herself.

"Thanks," she managed.

She turned the key and the big engine roared mercifully to life. Jocelyn sighed her relief and swallowed hard. She shifted into reverse and sort of nodded in Conti's direction but couldn't work up a smile.

"I'm going to follow you back," he said.

No! Don't! she wanted to shout, but she knew the tears would be sure to accompany that outburst, so she nodded again and hit the gas pedal. Dust and gravel flew up from her spin backward onto the highway. She realized too late that she hadn't looked to see if there were any cars coming. Fortunately, the road was as deserted as it had been when she arrived here what now seemed a lifetime ago.

She glanced back at the parking area and produce stand. Clint Conti might not have noticed her careless dash into the road because he was on his way to the pickup truck at the opposite side of the lot. She was, however, being observed by someone else. Davis Mapes was back in his kitchen chair by the wall of the vegetable stand, tilted onto the rear legs just as he had been when she'd first seen him earlier. He was staring straight at her. He had probably been staring straight at her ever since she came running down the hill. He lifted his hand in what the look in his eyes told her was a mock gesture of farewell.

Jocelyn shifted into drive and hit the gas pedal again. She didn't care if Conti saw her driving recklessly. She didn't care if he was following her or not. All she cared about was getting out of there and finding someplace where she could be alone to sort things through.

She glanced in the rearview mirror. Clint was following her, all right. Her burst of speed hadn't left him in the dust as she had hoped it might. The chrome of his truck's grillwork blinked back at her in the morning sunlight. He was going to trail her all the way to the campground. She would have to brush him off when they got there. She wasn't up to being around anybody just yet. She wondered if she was even up to brushing him off.

Why was he taking such a protective interest in her, anyway? She suspected this wasn't just his version of country hospitality. What was he doing out here on this remote Tug Hill road so early in the morning? She didn't believe in coincidences.

Then something happened that chased those questions straight out of her head. She had turned from the back road where the Mapes family lived to a slightly more primary route. To the left and off beyond a stand of trees a low ridge ran parallel to the road. That ridge was really not much taller than a hillock, but out here along this mostly flat plateau any elevation commanded attention. There was a break in the line of trees and a worn place wide enough for a car or truck to drive through to the wooded area beyond.

As she approached, Jocelyn saw a woman scurry out of the trees. When the woman saw the car, she hurried faster still, even though the pace was making her face visibly red. The woman began waving her arms so wildly that she stumbled and had to scramble back to her balance again. She was headed onto the road and straight into Jocelyn's path.

"What now?" Jocelyn sighed aloud.

She had no choice but to stop, though she did consider picking up speed and forging past. Let Conti take care of whatever this woman was after. Jocelyn was suddenly reminded of DeDe Mapes running behind this car just yesterday. Could this be another irate woman who had a personal bone to pick with Jocelyn? On second thought she doubted that. DeDe had been unmistakably angry. One look at this woman made it clear that she was just as unmistakably afraid. That was why Jocelyn had no choice but to stop.

She braked just as the woman was about to barrel straight into the car, as if she might have flung herself on the hood if Jocelyn hadn't decided to stop.

"Can I help you?" Jocelyn asked through her open window.

"I need a ride. I *desperately* need a ride."

To emphasize that point, she scurried around the front of the car to the passenger side and yanked open the door before Jocelyn had a chance to respond.

"Where are you going?" Jocelyn asked, wondering if she really wanted this distraught woman in her car.

"The same place you are. To the campground." She said this with some difficulty, being still out of breath from her mad dash out of the woods.

"You're at Tranquility?" Jocelyn didn't recall seeing her there, but she didn't know everybody at the campground, especially not this season's new arrivals.

"Yes, yes. I am. Can we get away from here now?" She was actually wringing her hands, between swipes to tuck a wild wisp of graying hair behind her ear.

"What happened to you? Why are you so frightened?"

"I promise I'll tell you if you will only take me away from here right this very minute."

Jocelyn could see that whether or not this woman's apparent terror might be justified, it was certainly real to her. If Jocelyn didn't do as her passenger pleaded, hysteria could be the result. She told her passenger to fasten her seat belt. A glance in the rearview mirror told her Clint had just pulled up behind her and was opening the door of his truck to get out.

Jocelyn didn't want to talk to him just now. She especially didn't want to talk to him about her personal life. Telling a tall handsome man that she hadn't been enough of a woman to hold on to her husband was the last thing she cared to do. She also didn't want Clint to know that she had been so stupid that she never even guessed that Philip had a girlfriend, much less a country love nest where he made his little rendezvous.

Suddenly, Jocelyn was so angry that she didn't think to ask herself why she should care what this stranger did or did not know about her. She gunned the Lincoln down the road, literally leaving Clint in her dust.

"Are you all right?" her passenger asked. She had stopped flipping her hair to stare at Jocelyn.

"You said you wanted to get out of here. I'm getting you out of here."

"Okay. Okay." The older woman looked as if she might have forsaken her former fear for a new one, of the wild-driving lady at the wheel of this big car.

Jocelyn knew how this must look to her passenger but didn't care. Jocelyn was beyond caring about much of anything, except her rabid desire to find Philip, in whatever dimension he might be at this moment, and sock him in the nose as hard as she could. Her foot leaped off the gas pedal. What a terrible thing to be thinking about! she admonished herself. Philip was dead!

The car had slowed to half its previous speed. Jocelyn's passenger put her hand on the door handle, as if she might be contemplating a fast escape. Jocelyn saw the gesture. For some reason it got through to her, penetrating her anger and guilt to the place where she could begin to think again.

"I'm sorry," Jocelyn said, loosening her grip on the wheel and correcting their speed to a normal pace. "I was thinking about something else."

"Yes, I could see that," said the passenger cautiously. She didn't let go of the door handle.

"My name is Jocelyn Wald. What's yours?" Jocelyn hoped that this most mundane of questions would set her passenger at ease.

"I'm Hildy Hammond."

"What are you doing at Tranquility? Are you there for the season?" Jocelyn had calmed down considerably, but she was still breathing erratically.

"I think it will be for the season, but I can't be sure. That will depend on how my project goes." Ms. Hammond turned from staring at Jocelyn to staring out the window. "Especially now."

"What kind of project are you working on?"

Ms. Hammond relaxed her stare only a little. "I am an anthropologist. I am doing a study of the precolonization population here and what their tribal activities were in this area."

"You're studying the local Indians?"

"We prefer to be referred to as native peoples," Hildy said, while managing not to sound at all pompous or belligerent.

"Are you a native American?" Jocelyn asked, making sure to be more politically correct this time.

"Only a fraction of me is, but doing this project seems to have brought me closer to that part. I wonder if what just happened has something to do with the awakening of that consciousness?"

Hildy had muttered that last question, as if to herself. Jocelyn responded, anyway. "What is it that just happened? Is that what scared you so much?"

"Yes, it is," Hildy said. "And I did promise I would tell you what was going on in return for a ride."

"That's right. You did."

Jocelyn was still personally shaken enough to wonder if she would be able to take in what Hildy had to say. Still, it might be a distraction. Jocelyn was willing to give it a try. Anything was better than thinking about Philip and DeDe and their house in the woods.

"I think I was visited by a spirit," Hildy said.

"What?" Jocelyn had been taken completely by surprise.

"I know how peculiar that sounds. It sounds peculiar to me as well."

Jocelyn glanced at Hildy Hammond. *Peculiar* was actually a good word for her. She was dressed in motley colors and materials, and there was mud on the knees of her pants and smudges on her shirt. Her round cheeks were no longer bright red, but her color was still high. Her hair was in disarray, and her swipes at the sides had only served to mat one strand against her head amid the undone rest.

"I was working in the quarry the same way I always do. There's a quarry back beyond the trees at the base of the ridge. I've been doing some digging there. I believe that area could be the site of a seasonal hunting ground that the Iroquois used year after year. Popular theory is that there was a battle fought here and that is why so many bones have been found. I don't agree. So, I've been digging for artifacts."

That would explain the muddy knees and smudged shirt.

"I had just found a particularly good shard that is most possibly Iroquois pottery." Hildy hesitated. "Then, it happened." She was staring toward the windshield again.

"What happened?" Hildy had managed to capture Jocelyn's attention, after all.

"I felt something." Hildy stopped herself. "Now, I have to think about this scientifically. I mustn't go flying off into conclusions like some featherbrained eccentric."

Jocelyn glanced over again. Along with *peculiar, featherbrained eccentric* might be another way of describing Hildy, at least in outward appearance.

"What kind of sensation was it exactly?" Hildy continued, obviously speaking more to herself than to Jocelyn. "A physical feeling, warm, not unpleasant, but urgent. Why urgent? Perhaps because it insisted on being noticed by me. As if I could have ignored it?"

"Ignored what? What are you talking about?"

"Oh, I'm sorry. I wander off like that on occasion, but usually only when I have a problem to solve. I will try to stay more in touch." Hildy actually chuckled at that. The tension in the car relaxed a bit. "Still, it's hard to say specifically what it is I'm talking about. Except that one minute I was digging, and the next I was . . . engulfed. That would describe it best. It was as if I had been suddenly surrounded by something—or someone. More accurate would be to say I was taken inside of that something rather than just surrounded by it. Now that I think about it calmly, it was actually not a bad feeling. Except for the urgency."

Jocelyn had been driving somewhat automatically, paying close attention to what Hildy was saying. This woman's story was too fantastic to be true. It reminded Jocelyn of the stuff her mother used to natter on about: the supernatural, horoscopes, readings, all that guff Jocelyn hated hearing.

"It sounds like a touch of heatstroke to me," she said.

Hildy looked over at Jocelyn and was thoughtful for a moment. "You could be right," she said. "That would certainly be a scientifically acceptable explanation."

With that, Hildy lapsed into silence. Jocelyn was grateful. Her entire life had just been shaken at its very foundation. The last thing she needed right now was to be forced to listen to some strange woman carry on about her paranormal experiences.

Fortunately, Hildy must have detected the lack of receptivity in her audience. Or possibly she simply didn't want to hear any more, even from herself, about whatever it was that had or had not happened to her at the quarry. She didn't say another word all the way back to Tranquility Campground.

CLINT CONTI had stuck to her like lint on wool, and she couldn't shake him off. She had tried waving at him before she turned into the trailer park. She had hoped he'd take the hint that she meant goodbye and continue on his way. No such luck. He followed her up the hill, then pulled over and waited while she dropped off Hildy at her site.

When Jocelyn got back here to her own trailer, she thanked Clint for his concern. She even gave him a farewell nod as she turned to walk away toward the deck. Still, he stood by his truck, watching her, as if to say, Don't think you're getting rid of me so easily.

He was walking toward her now. Her heart began to race in a way she didn't like at all. She would have liked to slide open the French doors, run inside and draw the drapes shut tight against his invasion of both her space and her emotions. But that would be rude. He was only trying to help. . . . Or was he?

He had reached the steps to the deck and said, as if echoing her thoughts, "Is there something I can help you with?"

"No, thank you. I'm just fine."

"You look anything but fine to me. Something happened to you back there at the Mapes place, and whatever it was has you pretty upset. I just want to know if there's anything I can do for you."

"I have to take care of this myself," Jocelyn said.

"I didn't offer to take the world off your hands, Jocelyn. I only asked if I could help you out a bit."

Jocelyn turned to stare at him. His words, or maybe the way he said them, struck through her confusion of emotions. There was a difference between handing your life over to somebody else and simply accepting some assistance along the way. Assistance was precisely what she needed right now. She wasn't too stubborn to admit that. Instinct told her she should trust him, if only a little.

"You know this area pretty well, don't you?" she said. "And you know the people, too."

"Well, I'm out of touch to some extent with the people. I've been away and haven't been back for very long."

"But you know who they are, and you know the countryside."

"Sure I do. I spent most of my life here. Why do you want to know?"

Jocelyn sighed. She still had doubts about doing this, but she was in a storm right now, or at least that's what it felt like. And this guy was the only port in sight.

"I do need your help," she said.

"I'll do whatever I can."

She looked at him for a moment. His eyes were green. She hadn't been able to tell last night in the firelight. Those eyes were also unmistakably sincere. Why did he care so much about her? Maybe he was simply a nice person. Maybe he had no ulterior motive. The longer she looked into his eyes, the more she felt herself wanting to believe that.

"Come on inside," she said. "We can talk more comfortably there."

The living room of her trailer was, in fact, very comfortable. A sofa with thick, soft cushions was set back into the bay window area opposite the French doors. Jocelyn gestured for Clint to sit down there while she took the single chair that faced the couch.

She wasn't at all sure how to go about saying this. Maybe it would be best to jump right in.

"You might say that my world got turned on end this morning," she began. "I found out some things that have given me quite a shock, and I need to make sure they are true. I suspect that they are, but I need to be absolutely certain."

"So, you would like me to help you check the situation out."

"That's right." She was grateful for his quick understanding.

"What is the situation, anyway?"

Her gratitude evaporated.

"If you're not ready to talk about it, we can wait till another time."

Jocelyn took a deep breath and exhaled forcefully. "No, I can talk about it now. Well, I don't really know if I can, I've just decided that I will."

She remained firm in that conviction, through every torturous word that followed. She told him about

Philip's death and a little about the months since. She took another deep breath before revealing that, unknown to her, Philip appeared to have been having an affair. She also told Clint that having met the woman involved, Jocelyn suspected that the relationship was something more than just a sexual liaison. She suspected that Philip had what you might call a separate life with this woman and that he had been about to leave Jocelyn for that other life the night he was killed.

Jocelyn didn't feel it necessary to mention how betrayed and humiliated she was feeling. She was pretty sure that showed quite clearly on her face. Clint's compassion for what she was going through was equally clear. His green eyes softened, and he leaned toward her across the coffee table. He reached out and touched her hand. She had never known a mere touch to feel so calming.

She continued telling her story until every agonizing word had been said. When that last word was spoken, she felt suddenly very, very tired. She walked Clint to the door. Then he did something she was totally unprepared for. He put his arms around her and folded her gently to him.

It was a natural gesture, considering the circumstances. She had revealed herself as sorely in need of comfort, and he was filling that need. Unfortunately, comfort was not what she felt in his arms, the unsettling, masculine scent of him all around her. A moment ago, she had been ready to collapse from exhaustion. Now, every nerve in her body snapped to attention. She pushed herself out of his embrace.

"I really have to be alone now," she said, no longer worried about whether she was being rude.

"I understand," he said, stepping outside.

An instant of panic gripped her. What if he really did understand? What if he knew that his arms around her nearly made her swoon like some silly heroine in a nineteenth-century novel? Furthermore, she had just confessed her history of trusting a man who was not worthy of that trust. Was she doing that again now? Did Clint Conti recognize her to be a bit of a fool in that department? Was he taking advantage of that foolishness?

She murmured a goodbye and was grateful beyond words when he nodded and walked away. The doors had barely slid shut behind him when Jocelyn made a dash for her bed and its bastion of pillows. Her exhaustion had returned. She didn't so much fall asleep as collapse into unconsciousness. She hardly moved, through the afternoon and beyond.

UNFORTUNATELY, JOCELYN did not awaken feeling refreshed. She came to with a hangover as strong as if she had been drugged into slumber. She stumbled out of bed and across the living room and kitchen areas to the compact bathroom that she had always thought of as endearing and cute. She had no such feelings now as she splashed her face with water and considered flinging herself, fully clothed, into the shower.

She might have done just that if she hadn't heard a sound that startled her almost to total wakefulness. Something had hit the side of the trailer, then brushed along it. Where it struck was too low for a tree branch. Besides, the roofed-in deck was on the other side of this wall. No tree branch could reach in there.

She heard the brushing sound again, this time moving down the wall in the direction of the French doors.

There was no mistaking it. Something was out there on her deck, in the dark.

Jocelyn might have been afraid, but her anger wouldn't allow it. She dashed out of the bathroom and down the short hallway past the wardrobe closet and into the kitchen. Intending to protect herself, she snatched something from the dinette table without really noticing what it was. After speeding across the living room carpet, she flung open the French doors.

It was a man, all right. He was crouched down and running away, so she couldn't really tell how tall he was or what he looked like. She thought he was wearing dark jeans, but she couldn't be absolutely sure. In fact, when she thought about it, he might not even be a man. Something seemed to be covering his head, maybe the hood of a sweatshirt. Jocelyn couldn't tell.

What she did know for sure was that she'd had enough. She stomped across the deck, hardly aware that she was in her bare feet. Standing at the top of the steps, she threw back her head and shouted, "Get away from here, and leave me alone, whoever you are. Or, so help me, I will kill you."

To punctuate her words, she brandished her weapon above her head. She was caught up in her rage, at this intruder, at Philip, at the unhappy turn of today's events. In fact, she was so taken over by her fury that she only half noticed that her weapon was a long-handled wooden spoon.

Chapter Five

The next morning came too soon for Jocelyn. It was very early on a gray, damp day—perfect for burrowing under the warm covers and drifting back to sleep. But she was wide awake.

Her nerves still rattled. She hadn't slept well. She had the feeling, more than the actual memory, that her dreams had been haunted by prowling, lurking, watching shadows she couldn't quite see into. She longed for peace of mind and wondered if she would ever have it again.

Maybe a night of exhausting lovemaking would do the trick.

That thought startled Jocelyn into even more agitation. Where had it come from? She hadn't thought about making love in months. She didn't even think about it much when Philip was alive. Heaven knows, nights with him hadn't been particularly exhausting.

Jocelyn clutched the comforter to her chest. Why was she thinking about this now? Of course, it was true that her sexual relationship with Philip hadn't been an especially passionate one. Still, she hadn't complained when he was alive. She shouldn't be dredging up their love life, or lack of such, now that he was dead.

I'll bet making love would be different with Clint Conti.

Jocelyn bolted straight up in bed. That thought had also come unbidden out of the blue. Though Clint Conti was an attractive man, she had met lots of attractive men in her life. She didn't necessarily start thinking about what they would be like in bed. Could it be that Clint was more attractive than the usual man, at least to her? Being in his arms, even for a moment, had been like nothing she had never known. How would it feel to have those arms around her forever?

She was doing it again! Letting her thoughts get out of control. She didn't know Clint Conti. She also had misgivings about him. How did he happen to be driving along that seldom-traveled Tug Hill road yesterday, just in time to chance upon her car at the Mapes place? Why did he stick to her like glue after that, as if they were closely connected even though she barely knew him? How did he know so much about her, and why would he care? Someone was definitely watching her, stalking her. Right now, he was the most likely suspect.

Jocelyn swung her legs over the side of the bed. She pulled on a blue ankle-length terry-cloth robe and buttoned it down the front while sliding her feet into matching slippers. She was about to shuffle into the kitchen to make coffee when she heard an unusual sound from outside. Immediately she recalled the brush of her intruder against the side of the trailer last night. This was different, though. It came from farther away. Actually, it sounded like someone mumbling.

Jocelyn stood up and tilted the slatted window a bit farther open. The morning was a gray one, all right. A light rain fell steadily. The leaves on a nearby branch were heavy with moisture. The sky was low and misty with the thick, gray-white clouds seeming to touch the tops of the trees. There were fewer bird sounds than on more pleasant mornings. Maybe that was why she had noticed the mumbling.

Grumbling would be a more accurate description; and it came from the campsite beyond the road. There hadn't been anyone camped there yesterday. In fact, that site was generally one of the last to be filled. The Delaneys considered it an overflow site, and besides, they had always tried to indulge the Walds' preference for privacy. But there was someone on that site this morning, even though the campground was hardly filled to overflowing. Jocelyn had noticed lots of unoccupied sites, more than usual for this time of year.

The Delaneys had the right to locate people wherever they wanted. Jocelyn didn't question that. All the same, she was surprised. As she watched her new neighbor for a moment longer, she became concerned, as well.

He was less than six feet tall and of spare, wiry build. He was wearing an olive green army fatigue jacket and the inevitable jeans that were so much a uniform of summer camping life. His hair was short in tight waves that appeared to grow curlier by the second as the rain settled on him. He was trying to attach corner poles to the awning that pulled out from the side of his small recreation vehicle.

Rain had settled in the sagging pocket at the center of the awning, and the weight of the water was impairing his progress with the poles. He had obviously not mastered the concept of angling the poles and driving their points into the ground to give the awning stability. Even more obvious was that this man was as much a greenhorn camper as Jocelyn had ever seen.

He was also frustrated, and the way he expressed that frustration made Jocelyn more than a little uneasy. He was talking to himself, or perhaps to the awning, carrying on about how badly the work was going. Jocelyn couldn't make out the exact words, but the tone was definitely disgruntled. He even shook his fist heavenward a couple of times, either at the continuing rainfall or the creator of that rainfall farther above. This was eccentric behavior, of course, but not in itself alarming.

What Jocelyn found unsettling was how vehemently he wrestled with the awning's ropes and poles. His movements reflected intensifying anger at two chrome poles and a few yards of line. He shook the poles angrily as if he intended to bully them into place. He yanked at the lines and, thus, twisted them more tightly in the least effective direction. His face was beet red and wore a sheen of perspiration as well as raindrops. Jocelyn could see that he was working himself into a rage.

The ground beneath his running shoes was being trampled into mud by his frantic treading back and forth between the poles. It was inevitable that he would slip eventually, and he did. That was most likely what triggered his next irrational act and the result that followed.

He fell to one knee and had to brace himself by slamming a hand into the mud to keep himself from falling all the way down. He jumped to his feet again and glared down at his muddy jeans and sneakers. He looked around for somewhere to wipe his muddy palm but found nothing. That final frustration must have been too much for him to bear. He balled his muddy fist and, amid loud grumblings that now sounded more like curses, he hauled off and socked one of the chrome poles full force.

For a split second the pole and the awning appeared to be suspended in stunned inertia, as if they could hardly believe what this man had just done. Then the response came. Though Jocelyn would have liked to call out and warn the man of what was going on, there was no time. Before she could get her mouth open to holler, the pole was falling, the awning edge was dipping, and the puddle of water had dumped itself over the rim, straight onto the man's head.

Ordinarily, Jocelyn would probably have laughed, not in a meanspirited way, but simply because of the pure slapstick of the scene. One look at the man's face froze the laughter in her throat. His cheeks were stained redder still, but that wasn't what struck a chill in her bones that had nothing to do with the rainy morning. What made her shudder was the expression on his face.

Jocelyn had never seen anyone so furious, not that she could remember, anyway. Even more startling, she had never seen a look this cruel. His features were distorted by it. His eyes disappeared behind menacing slits. His mouth was twisted with what Jocelyn had to identify as hatred, and he was no longer grumbling. Now, he was snarling.

Jocelyn was suddenly very uncomfortable watching this man, whoever he might be. She pushed at the window slat to close it, but the slat wouldn't move. She glanced out again, just as the man stopped dead still amid his gesticulations to stare straight back at her. The expression on his face softened only a little. He stood there, with the puddled rainwater still dripping out of his hair onto his shoulders, glowering across the yards of road and grass between them. It was clear that he had discovered her watching him and that he wasn't pleased.

Jocelyn gave the slat one more tug. When it still didn't budge, she hurried away from the window and out of the bedroom. She practically ran across the living room area and into the kitchen. She pressed her back against the edge of the sink and listened intently. Both the grumbling and the snarling had ceased. She strained to hear some other sound that might tell her what her distraught and scary neighbor was doing now. This concentration on the auditory senses could have been the reason that the knock on her door sounded much louder than it really was and made her jump when she heard it.

Jocelyn stared at the wide doorway. The heavy drapes were still drawn across the glass. She wished she could see through them to whoever was standing on the other side. Could it be the man from the campsite across the road? If so, why would he come here? She turned toward the sink and lifted the corner of the window curtain above it. A tree obscured her view, but she could make out the front of the neighboring trailer through the leaves and branches. The man was no longer there.

The knock came at the door again, nowhere near as loud as she had imagined it to be the first time.

"Miss," a man called from Jocelyn's deck.

She didn't recognize the voice, and she didn't answer.

"My name is Sonny Shannon. I'm from the RV across the way," he said. "I guess you saw my little rain dance over there. I stopped over to introduce myself and show you I'm not as crazy as I look."

His tone was jovial. He hardly sounded as if he could be the angry man she'd watched through the window just moments ago. She felt a little foolish cowering behind the drapes in here. Still, she would use her common sense and keep the screen locked between them. Jocelyn walked across the carpeted living room area to the French doors. She drew the drapes aside, and there he was. His smile was as wide and jolly as his scowl had been menacing before. She only slid the door open wide enough to talk through and held on to the handle so she could slam it shut if she needed to.

"Hi," he said as his smile spread even wider. "I'm Sonny Shannon," he repeated.

Jocelyn had the feeling he was about to extend his hand for a shake. If he did, she would have to decide whether to open the screen door and be hospitable or leave it closed and remain cautious. Fortunately, he kept his hands in the pockets of his fatigue jacket.

"I'm Jocelyn Wald," she replied and smiled back, though not anywhere near as broadly as he had.

"I feel a little sheepish about having you see me stumbling around out there pretending I know what I'm doing."

"Is this your first time camping?"

"I bet you guessed that right away," he said with a chuckle at himself. "It was also my first time being attacked by an awning. And the awning won."

Jocelyn couldn't help but chuckle along with him this time. "We all have to start somewhere. I've had my own share of mishaps out here." Though she couldn't recall ever being as clumsy as he appeared to be.

"My cousin left this camper behind when he went in the service, and I thought I'd give it a shot. I'm bound to get the hang of it or drown trying."

He ran his fingers through his very wet hair. There were dark marks on the shoulders of his jacket where the rainwater had soaked through. A really good neighbor would invite him in and brew some hot coffee for him while he dried off. But there had been something in his snarling face earlier that tripped a warning alarm in Jocelyn's psyche. She wasn't inclined to ignore that instinct now. She didn't know anything about this man, except that he appeared to be about as well adapted to the outdoors as a fish is to the beach. Still, she didn't like to think of him contracting pneumonia just because he didn't happen to be a woodsman.

"Do you have a heater in there?" She nodded backward in the direction of his trailer.

"According to the instruction book I do." He hesitated a moment, as if he might be waiting for that invitation to morning coffee.

Jocelyn didn't oblige him. "Don't be surprised if it takes two or three tries to get it lit. They require a bit of getting used to."

"Well, I'd better be at it, then. If I explode the place out from under me, you'll be able to report what happened." He backed toward the steps in a reluctant gait.

Jocelyn suspected this to be a final plea for a coffee reprieve. Though his sense of humor had warmed her to him some, she wasn't ready to let him inside here with her. "Good luck" was all she said in reply.

He pulled one hand out of a pocket and touched his forehead in a jaunty salute. His smile had narrowed only slightly as he took off at a jog around the corner of her long trailer toward his much smaller one.

Jocelyn slid the glass door closed against the rainy dampness, then set about opening curtains and drapes to let in whatever light this gloomy morning had to offer. She kept the blinds slanted nearly shut on the side facing Sonny Shannon's RV. Because of the weather, she wouldn't be spending her morning on the deck as usual. If she was going to be inside, she would prefer to do so in privacy, especially since she still had questions about her new neighbor's character and intentions.

As she went about turning on lights to brighten the gloom and lighting the heater to dry off the dampness, she was half listening for the blast Mr. Shannon had jokingly anticipated—or for the sound of his grumbling resumed. Fortunately, all remained quiet from across the road.

THE NEXT KNOCK didn't come until Jocelyn had a chance to dress in comfortably soft jeans and an equally comfortable cotton sweater, which was heavy enough to ward off any chill from the earlier rain. That rain had stopped by now, though the sky remained cloudy and the grass had not yet dried off.

Meanwhile, the coffee was made, and she had baked some muffins in the oven so the trailer smelled like bursting blueberries. The heater was at its lowest setting since it wasn't really cold outside, but Jocelyn still preferred the coziness of some warmth on a damp day.

That coziness dispelled whatever uneasiness she had felt as a result of her strange meeting with Sonny Shannon. She was even somewhat grateful to him for having taken her mind off her real problems, if only for a brief while. When she saw who was knocking at her windowed door, that respite came to an end. She vaguely remembered Clint Conti's saying he would be here this morning. Or was she the one who had asked him to come? Whichever it had been, he was true to his word and standing on her deck at this very moment. She sighed as she slid the door open and unlatched the screen.

"Someone certainly made a muddy mess out here," Clint said. "Were you tramping around in the rain to wake yourself up this morning?"

Jocelyn surveyed the deck floor where Sonny Shannon's muddy sneakers had left their unmistakable tread marks both on and off the rubber mat where Clint was now wiping his booted feet.

"My new neighbor stopped over to introduce himself," she replied, stepping aside so Clint could come in.

He hesitated on the doorstep. "Would you like me to take these off?" He gestured toward his boots. "They might have some mud left on them."

"Don't worry about that," she said, motioning for him to step inside.

He brushed past her, and she knew instantly that she wanted him here, after all. She pulled the screen shut but left the door ajar to let in the gradually warming morning air. There was no getting around it. She was very attracted to this man, and the new Jocelyn wasn't going to hide from that fact. What he made her feel might be unsettling in its storminess, but she was determined to ride it out.

"That's what's so great about this life-style," she said. "You don't have to bother yourself about a little mud. I just let it dry, then sweep it out the door." She couldn't help thinking that other problems weren't so easy to get rid of.

"You've made this place so attractive," he said, looking around. "I noticed that yesterday. I wouldn't want to mess it up on you."

"It's designed for comfort as well as beauty. In fact, I could probably live in this trailer year-round if it was somewhere warm during the winter months."

"I would have thought this life was too basic for somebody like you full-time. It would be for a lot of women."

"I don't think of this as basic." Jocelyn smiled as she looked around at the microwave, full convection oven, well-stocked refrigerator-freezer and cable-ready TV. She was also smiling because she was feeling a bit more at ease with him.

"You have a point there," he said, taking a seat at the kitchen dinette table. "You can't get fresh-baked muffins out of an L. L. Bean tent. And if you don't recognize that as a hint, I need to brush up on my skills."

Jocelyn smiled again as she lifted the towel from the covered basket and took out two plump muffins that were still fragrantly warm. She poured a cup of coffee and couldn't help thinking how pleasant it felt to be playing hostess to a handsome man in her little summer home. Without warning, that thought inspired another one, of how she had been wondering just this morning about what it would be like to make love to this same handsome man. Jocelyn's hand shook slightly. The cup rattled against its saucer, making her wish she had put the coffee in a mug instead.

"Can I help you with that?" Clint asked.

"No, thanks. I've got everything under control."

Jocelyn did her best to compose herself as she carried the muffins and coffee to the table. She also decided it would be wise to take some of the coziness out of this little domestic scene. She might have resolved to wait out the storm of her attraction to Clint, but she wasn't ready to set up housekeeping with him in the meantime. The scenario of the lonely widow desperate for a man in her bed and board came to mind and wasn't to Jocelyn's liking.

"Have you ever heard of a man named Sonny Shannon?" she asked, moving the subject to less personal territory.

"Sure. I know Sonny. Where did you run into him?"

"He's the new neighbor I told you about. His RV is parked across the road."

"I saw that there and wondered about it. The Delaneys generally try to keep that site empty for you if they can manage it. Sonny never struck me as the type for roughing it, either."

Jocelyn laughed. "You can say that again. He was all thumbs trying to keep the rain off himself this morning."

"Sonny's a bit of a character. I wouldn't be surprised by any antics he pulled."

"I noticed that about him, too."

"He's a good guy, though. He's also a cop. That's how I know him mostly, except for sports. We went to different schools and ended up playing against each other all year long. Football, basketball, baseball. In these small town high schools up here you get to play them all."

Jocelyn told herself she would not think about how well suited Clint's muscular body would be to athletics. At least she wouldn't think about that right now.

"So Sonny Shannon is a cop," she said. "State or local?"

"He's with the sheriff's department." Clint hesitated for a moment, contemplating his coffee cup. "My brother Patrick was with the department, too."

"Then he should know Shannon pretty well."

"He *knew* him. Patrick was killed last year."

"I'm sorry to hear that," Jocelyn said.

"That's okay," he said unconvincingly. He sounded as if he didn't want to discuss it further.

"Anyway, maybe the Delaneys can move Shannon if you'd like your privacy back."

"That's not necessary," she said quickly. "He's not bothering me."

"We want you to be as comfortable as possible while you're up here in the north country."

There was something about the way he said that and the warm smile in his eyes that told Jocelyn they were straying into too intimate territory again.

"I have somewhere I would like to go today," she said quickly. "It has to do with Philip. Maybe you could come along. I have a feeling you might be of help."

"A game plan? Sounds good to me," Clint said, between mouthfuls of muffin. "What did you have in mind?"

"I'd like to go to the airport that Philip used. It's over near Adams. Do you know where I mean?"

"Sure. I used to hang out around there when I was younger. A lot of the local guys did. What do you think you'll find out there?"

"I don't know really, but Philip spent quite a bit of time there." Jocelyn turned toward the sink and occupied herself with the few dishes so she wouldn't have to look at Clint. "DeDe Mapes told me that's where she met Philip."

"I see." Clint finished his coffee and brought his cup, saucer and muffin plate to the sink where Jocelyn was still pretending to be absorbed in what she was doing. He laid his hand on her shoulder gently, but it startled her, anyway. "By the way, you bake a mean muffin, Miss Jocelyn. I don't know when I've enjoyed a breakfast more."

"Thanks," she said. She wanted to move away from his touch but couldn't.

He patted her shoulder before removing his hand. "Now we had better get on the road so we can be at the airport while the Saturday regulars are still around."

Jocelyn nodded but didn't say anything. She wished she was more certain she was doing the right thing by accepting Clint's help. She wasn't really worried about his trying to take matters out of her hands and run them himself the way Philip would have done. She already sensed Clint was a different kind of man. He would respect her wishes and follow her lead if she wanted him to. But would she want him to? Would she be too tempted to fall into the old patterns of dependence? More troubling still, was this a man she should be depending on? Her suspicions might have quieted some, but they had not disappeared altogether. Still, she was shaky enough from the events of the past two days to be grateful to have someone with her while she went sleuthing today.

As for her feelings toward Clint and whether a relationship with him would be wise right now, she would set those considerations aside for the time being. Right now, she needed to solve some mysteries about Philip and her past life. There could be no future for her, with or without Clint Conti, until that had been done.

Chapter Six

The Lewis-Adams Airport was little more than a long, wide field with a concrete runway down the middle of it. Two hangars and a small building with a tower on top were the only structures on the premises. Ordinarily, there would have been the handful of regulars Clint had mentioned, a couple of pilots, and that would be all. But this Saturday there was a flea market. The area from behind the hangars to the road had been measured off in rows of stands and tables with a walking path between for browsers.

On most any other occasion, Jocelyn would have joined that rambling crowd to pick through the assortment of jewelry pieces, used books, discount cosmetics and bric-a-brac. She enjoyed the prospect of finding that precious gem among the odds and ends that made such excursions more of a treasure hunt than a browse. Today, however, she was looking for something very different, and it was not likely to turn out to be a treasure.

On the other side of the hangars was the runway. Parked along its length, beyond the hangars, were the planes. They were all small, though varying widely in age and condition. Some were nearly new and brightly painted in sparkling color combinations. Others were older and less impressive, some with dents and scratches along their sides and cracked leather upholstery inside. Most appeared to be currently functional, whatever their physical condition. Only in the very back row and farthest from the hangars could any tall grass be seen to have grown around the wheels or where the tail touched the ground.

Nearby, inside one hangar was a single small jet-engine type similar to the one Philip had flown. The runway had been lengthened considerably a few years ago to accommodate these more powerful aircraft. There were only a handful using the facility, mostly well-to-do hunters traveling north to the hunting lodges in the fall.

Jocelyn and Clint walked through the flea market to get to the hangars. They were watched with curiosity along the way. She was aware of that but not alarmed. Her experience of northern New Yorkers was that they did not let much escape their notice. That was part of their cautious nature. Jocelyn had the theory that a history of hard winters made them hesitant to expect the best of anything or anyone.

A day might dawn with sunshine. Then, by midday, a blizzard could buffet you off the road and bury you. That possibility could make anybody skeptical of appearances eventually. Still, Jocelyn would have preferred to have their stares directed elsewhere, especially since she suspected they were wondering why she and Clint were together.

A stretch of tall grasses separated the scrubby field of the flea market from the hangar area. The ground was still soft from the rain, even marshy in places where Jocelyn guessed there would have been pussy willows and cattails growing back in springtime. She knew this country well enough to have worn her high black waterproof boots stuffed up under the legs of her jeans. She could slog through the watery sections without worrying about going home with wet feet.

The day had warmed up considerably, so she had changed her summer sweater for a T-shirt with a lightweight anorak over it in case it should turn rainy again. Jocelyn had become as cautious as the natives where the weather was concerned.

They had trekked halfway across the grassy stretch when Jocelyn became aware of someone else watching them, but not from the flea market behind them this time. This observer lounged against the door to the nearest hangar and stared directly at Jocelyn and Clint as they approached him. The closer they came, the more familiar he looked to Jocelyn. Finally, she knew why.

"Do you see that guy leaning against the building and watching us?" she asked Clint.

"How could I miss him?"

"Would he be Davis Mapes's brother by any chance?"

"Sure is. The Mapeses all look alike, except for DeDe. She—" He stopped himself from saying more and glanced uneasily toward Jocelyn, as if he had momentarily forgotten that the subject of Philip's former lover was delicate territory.

"Except that DeDe is too pretty to look like her brothers," Jocelyn completed the statement for him. "I had noticed that myself, Clint. You don't have to feel awkward about saying it."

Clint nodded and was silent for a moment. "You are more than pretty, if you ask me. In fact, you're beautiful."

Jocelyn looked up at him. She couldn't think what she should say in response to that. She wasn't accustomed to compliments on her appearance. Philip hardly even mentioned it.

"Of course, you didn't ask me, so I probably should keep my mouth shut," Clint said when her lack of response began to feel awkward.

"Not at all," she said. "I'm the one who should learn how to open her mouth and say thank you."

"You're welcome."

"So, is this the Mapes brother named Dolby?" she asked, mostly to change the subject.

"That's Dolby, all right."

"DeDe told me he hangs around out here trying to pick up odd jobs. He's the one who introduced her to Philip."

The resemblance between Davis and Dolby was strong in their facial features. They both had heavy bones and brows and small, slitted eyes. They were also about the same height, but much different in physique. Davis had been broad in the chest and shoulders. He obviously spent a lot of time either working out or working hard. Dolby, on the other hand, was much thinner and not the least bit muscular. His dark T-shirt hung loosely from narrow shoulders and a concave chest.

Nonetheless, Dolby was much more sinister than his brother had been. There was something more menacing than simple surliness in Dolby's eyes. He was angry, and that anger had a dangerous edge to it. Jocelyn recognized that ever more clearly as the distance between them lessened. She also couldn't help feeling that his anger was directed specifically at her. That impression was so distinct that she had to turn her gaze deliberately away from him, as if she feared being seared by the heat of his animosity.

If Clint noticed any of that about Dolby, it wasn't apparent in their greeting to each other. They said deep-voiced hellos and exchanged one of those very male handshakes that involves a lot of hard gripping and showing of the knuckles.

"What are you doing out here, man?" Dolby asked, neither looking at Jocelyn nor acknowledging her presence in any way. "Scouting out bargains over there at the junk tables?" He nodded toward the flea market.

"One person's junk is somebody else's treasure," Clint answered.

"I wouldn't know about that, man. I ain't had much experience with treasure." The bitterness in Dolby's tone matched the anger Jocelyn had seen in his eyes. "I do know that these yuppie types show up from the city every now and then thinkin' they're going to put one over on us stupid country hicks." He still didn't look at Jocelyn, but she had no doubt that he was referring to her.

Clint must have had the same impression. "You wouldn't be talking about Mrs. Wald, would you, Dolby?" he asked, sounding a little menacing himself.

"What if I was?"

"It wouldn't be polite, that's all. We wouldn't want anybody to get the idea that north country people aren't polite."

"What if I don't care what anybody thinks, especially not a certain somebody? You want to do something about it, like have a fight about it, maybe?"

Dolby flexed his skinny shoulders into an even more belligerent pose. He might not be anywhere near Clint's size or girth, but Dolby had bared his teeth in a manner that suggested he might try to gnaw his way through an opponent if other methods of combat didn't work out.

Meanwhile, Jocelyn could hardly believe that she was standing here watching this display of testosterone-driven posturing. These two men were actually squaring off against each other like stags on a mountainside, or was that rams on a cliff edge? Whatever the parallel behavior in nature might be, it was further down the evolutionary chain than she wanted to make her personal acquaintance. She was seriously thinking about walking away from what she considered a barbaric spectacle. Then Clint shrugged, and that simple movement defused the tension.

"You know me, Dolby," he said. "I'm not one to look for a battle if I can help it."

"I know you mostly by reputation, man," Dolby said as his scowl slid into an unpleasant smile. "The way I remember it, they used to say that you were more of a lover than a fighter."

Dolby glanced toward Jocelyn with a suggestive leer. You can't convict somebody for a nasty look, but for an instant she wished Clint hadn't backed off from the prospect of fighting this guy. Maybe Clint would have knocked Dolby's teeth out so the little weasel wouldn't be likely to gnaw his way through so much as a slice of bread for a while.

"Have you met Jocelyn Wald?" Clint asked.

"I know who she is." Dolby cast his slitted glance sideways at Jocelyn for a moment. He didn't bother either to smile or offer her a greeting. "I also know what happened yesterday. I hear she found out some bad news about her dead husband."

"What bad news would that be?" Clint asked, obviously fishing to find out just how much Dolby might have heard.

"I know that the missus here found out her old man was gettin' it on with my sister. Did you know I'm the one who got that started? Did you know I'm the one that introduced them?"

He sneered gleefully at Jocelyn as he asked those questions. She tried to defray the hurt of what he was saying by wondering how somebody she had never met before could harbor such personal bitterness toward her. Then she saw Clint step forward and raise his arm to grab Dolby. She took Clint's hand before he could do that.

"I know that you introduced DeDe to my husband," Jocelyn said to Dolby. "I have no hard feelings about that, toward either you or your sister. She is a lovely young woman, and I believe she truly cared for Philip, or Reggie, as you knew him. Any fault that there is in all of this belongs with him. And maybe with me."

Clint had turned her hand in his so that the clasp was comforting now. She was glad to feel his support, but, oddly enough, she suddenly didn't require as much comfort and support as she had thought she did.

Saying out loud the words she had just spoken to Dolby Mapes had freed her somehow, perhaps from the anguish of searching for somebody to blame. For now what she needed was to find out the truth about

Philip. Only then would she be able to determine the truth about herself. There would be more revelations to come, very possibly some painful ones, but from this moment on, however, she was sure that pain would not be devastating. She had Dolby to thank, at least in part, for that realization.

"I will understand if you don't want to help me," she said, "but I would appreciate anything you can tell me about my late husband and his dealings here."

Maybe it was the softness of her voice that did it. Dolby's eyes had lost some of their angry glint. He cleared his throat and squinted off into the partly cloudy distance for a long moment before answering.

"I'll take you to meet Charlie Gillis," he said finally. "He's the one to ask about Reggie Williams. Your husband, that is."

"Thank you, Dolby. I'd be grateful for that," Jocelyn said.

Dolby started off toward the other hangar. Jocelyn and Clint followed, and he did not let go of her hand.

CHARLIE GILLIS was an airplane mechanic, and a good one, from what Dolby said. Charlie also already knew about Reggie Williams's other identity.

"A story like that spreads faster than oil in August," Charlie said. "You'd have to expect that. Especially around a place like this where we can get hard up for excitement sometimes. You'll be lucky if it doesn't end up in the *Gazette*."

Jocelyn sighed. "I hope not."

"I think Charlie's exaggerating some," Clint said. "The *Lewis County Gazette* may only be a small-town weekly, but they are not about to print uncorroborated gossip."

"Are you tryin' to say my sister is a liar?" Dolby sounded as if he might be sharpening his angry edge again.

"I'm not saying that at all," Clint replied. "It's just that the circumstances would have to be investigated and the details proven to be factual before a reputable paper would take a chance on reporting such a sensational story. And there isn't going to be any such investigation."

"Yes, there is," Jocelyn said.

Her words struck the three men silent as they all turned to stare at her.

"I intend to conduct exactly that kind of investigation myself, and whatever I find out will be made available to DeDe Mapes. She can do what she wants with it. If she wants to put the story in the paper or hire one of those planes out there to write it across the sky, that's her choice." Jocelyn hadn't meant to be quite so vehement. It simply came out that way. "As for me, I don't think I will be staying around here, anyway. Probably not much longer than it takes to get to the bottom of things."

Clint had been standing at her side. Now he stepped back from her with a troubled expression on his face.

"Well, I'll be damned" was all Dolby Mapes had to say, shaking his head in amazement.

Charlie Gillis was wiping his hands vigorously on a towel that was already very greasy. "Why don't you let sleeping dogs lie?" he asked. "What good can come out of dredging up a lot of bad news? Nobody's going to profit by it."

"She told you, Charlie. She wants to get at the truth," Dolby piped in.

"Let the dead bury the dead," Charlie said. "And I *don't* believe I'm going to help you rake through the ashes of this one. Reggie treated me all right, and I'm not sharing his business with anybody."

"If he treated you so damned nice, how come you was fightin' him a couple of weeks before he bought it?" Dolby asked.

"I don't know what you're talking about," Charlie protested, throwing his rag on the stained floor of the hangar. "I don't remember any fight. And what if Reggie and I did have words? Everybody has words once in a while. That doesn't mean they're not still buddies, and I don't tell tales on a buddy."

He turned to walk away from them, but Jocelyn stepped forward and put her hand on his arm to stop him. "I respect your scruples, Mr. Gillis," she began.

Dolby snorted. "Scruples? Charlie wouldn't know a scruple if it fell on his head."

"Please, Dolby, let me handle this," Jocelyn said. "As I was saying, Mr. Gillis, I would simply like to know if there was anything out of the ordinary about my husband's activities here."

"What do you mean by out of the ordinary?" Charlie asked, regarding her suspiciously.

"He would fly in from Syracuse on Fridays some weekends. Then he would fly back to Syracuse on Sundays. Was that all he did here?"

Charlie thought for a moment before answering. "He'd go up for a spin on Saturday afternoons sometimes. That's all I know about."

He did walk away this time, in the direction of the tool bench that stretched along the hangar wall. Before he could get more than a couple of yards, Dolby headed him off.

"That's not all Williams did around here, and you know it, Charlie," Dolby said.

"Are you calling me a liar?" Charlie reached out his arm to sweep Dolby aside.

"Yes, I am." Dolby grabbed that arm. Though he was a head shorter than Charlie and skinny as a rail, there must have been power in his grip because Charlie's arm trembled from exertion but didn't move. "Tell her about the other trips Reggie made. The ones he took out of here on Saturdays about once a month."

"You don't know what you're talking about," Charlie said, trying to pull his arm free.

Dolby didn't let go. "I know what I'm talkin' about, all right. My sister went along on a couple of those trips, and I made it my business to find out about the others. I even know where he was goin' on those flights."

Charlie gave his arm a hard yank and wrenched it away from Dolby. "Then what did you bother coming around here bothering me for? Why didn't you just tell them what you think you know yourself?"

"Because I thought you could show them the solid evidence. Flight charts and like that." Dolby wiped his hand on the leg of his black jeans to get rid of the grease from Charlie's arm.

"I'm not showing anybody any flight records unless I see a warrant. Those are private papers, especially for a guy that's dead already."

"Please, Dolby," Jocelyn pleaded. "Just tell me what you know. I don't need to see charts and records. I'll take your word, and DeDe's."

Dolby looked pleased by that. "Well, as I said, she went with Reggie on a couple of those trips of his. He went to the same place both times. I snuck a look at the flight plans he filed for his other Saturday flights and the mileage when he got back. He always went the same distance and filed for the same destination."

"What destination was that?" Clint asked. He had stepped back to Jocelyn's side. Now he put a protective arm around her.

"New York City. Reggie would fly to New York City," Dolby said. "Ain't that right, Charlie?"

Charlie had gone to the workbench. He stood there puttering with some oily engine parts and did not acknowledge hearing the question, though he must have.

"Are you sure about that destination?" Jocelyn asked Dolby. "Are you sure it was New York City?" She sounded as bewildered as she felt.

"Sure as shootin'. You can ask DeDe. She'll tell you. They went once when they were gone for the whole day. He took her to meet some cronies of his there. She talked about it for days afterward."

There had been a Saturday when Philip was gone from the trailer all day. As Jocelyn remembered it, he said he had been working on the fuel line of the plane and lost track of the time. There were other weekends he had been gone several hours at a stretch. It would only take an hour and a half or so to fly to New York from here, maybe even less in Philip's plane, which was pretty fast. Still, she was confused.

"What's wrong, Jocelyn?" Clint asked. "Do you have some reason to question what Dolby's saying?"

"It's just that Philip hated New York City. He told me he wouldn't go there if his life depended on it."

But then Philip had also told her he wouldn't want a house in the north country if it were the last place on earth left to live.

JOCELYN DIDN'T WANT to walk back through the flea market. All those stares and heads-together whispers. She would rather not inflict that on herself right now. Besides, her rain boots were becoming uncomfortable in the steadily warming day. The sun had come out from behind the thinning clouds and was turning the moisture from the marsh to humidity all around them. She pulled off her jacket and tied the sleeves around her waist. She would have liked to strip off her boots, as well, and toddle barefoot back to the truck. There would be enough stares without that.

She could ask Clint to walk around the market area, but that was two or three times the distance of going straight through. That wouldn't have been so bad if it weren't for her clammy boots and the sock that had begun to creep down and bunch up behind her right ankle. She shuffled out of the tall grasses with Clint and began the trek down the gauntlet of prying eyes that led to the road.

"Well, if it isn't my old friend Conti."

The voice came from behind a table with a display of hunting knives, handcuffs, brass knuckles, Harley Davidson belt buckles and other emblems and instruments of violence. Jocelyn could hardly look at the stuff, and she certainly didn't want to talk to the kind of guy who would put together such a collection.

Something else was bothering her. It was more than just a sensation of being watched. With all those pairs of eyes on her, she could hardly have felt anything but watched. She had seen something else, too, or thought she saw something, out of the corner of her eye, appearing then disappearing a couple of rows of tables away from where they were walking. She was about to take a closer look when Clint took her elbow and began pulling her along at a faster pace.

"Hey, Conti," the rough voice shouted after them from the knife table. "Looks like running away runs in your family. Isn't that what your little brother was doing when he took a header into that tree last year?"

Clint stopped so abruptly that Jocelyn almost stumbled. She was glad not to be racing along anymore, for her bunched-up sock chafed the bottom of her foot with each step. She wasn't glad to be part of a potentially volatile scene, though.

Clint's grip had tightened on her arm. She guessed he didn't realize just how powerfully he had locked her in his grasp. He had tensed all over, probably in a struggle to maintain control. His muscles rippled into steely plates and hardened there. She was about to protest that he was hurting her, when his fingers suddenly relaxed, and she was able to slip her arm away from him. She was certain he would turn around and confront his tormentor. But Clint didn't move.

A hush had fallen over the crowd and the vendors. Even the guy who ran the bootlegged-tape-and-CD booth and played golden oldies and country-western all day long switched the music off to listen to what was going on. The faces turned toward Clint were expectant. They wanted some excitement out of this increasingly oppressive day. They hoped Clint would oblige.

Jocelyn, however, wasn't looking at Clint. Her attention was on his adversary. More precisely, her attention was riveted on the object bobbing from his left earlobe. It was a silver skull, particularly detailed in the gauntness of its cheeks and the empty hollows of its eye sockets. She stared at its spectral grin as if she might be staring into the face of evil itself.

"Too yellow to give me an answer to that one, aren't you, Conti?" jeered the wearer of the skull. "Just like little brother Patrick was too yellow to stick around and face the music when it was playing for him instead of all the other guys he railroaded."

Clint turned slowly around, as if he were on a pivot or a revolving platform at an exhibition and what he had to exhibit was raw, barely constrained fury.

"You know what my answer is to that, Rango," he said in a voice so low that it was really a growl.

Rango continued to sneer. A half dozen burly men Jocelyn assumed to be his buddies had lined up behind him like a wall of mean muscle.

Suddenly Jocelyn's instincts warned her there was something else going on here, too.

She glanced quickly around from the spot two rows away where she had thought she saw a lurking form to the periphery of the flat mowed area on the road side of the flea market field. Off in that direction was another stand of tall grasses bordering a ditch that paralleled the road. Jocelyn saw something part the grasses, then disappear among them. It could have been a big dog, but she didn't think so. Yet, if it were a person, he would have to have been crouched very low to duck out of sight that way.

In the meantime, Rango had taken a long step forward, and his phalanx moved with him.

"Yeah, Conti. I know what you're gonna say." Rango matched his growl to Clint's. "You're gonna say that little brother Patrick was framed."

"That's right," Clint answered. "He was framed."

Rango jerked his head back and barked a laugh that could never have been mistaken for mirthful. Then he snapped his glare toward Clint once more.

"That's what I said when that scumbag brother of yours took me in on the bum rap that got me put away five years ago," Rango snarled. "He called me a liar then, and I'm calling you a liar now. What are you going to do about it?"

Jocelyn looked up at Clint. The set of his jaw was so rigid that his teeth must have been grinding. A small muscle worked slightly in the hollow of his cheek, but otherwise his features might have been set in stone. She watched him look from one of Rango's henchmen to the next, then the next, locking on to each one's stare in turn before passing on. When he had come to the end of that forbidding lineup, Clint stared off into space for a moment. Then he breathed a sigh so barely perceptible that Jocelyn might have missed it had she not been watching him so closely.

"Nothing," Clint said. "I'm not going to do anything about it."

His words hung in silence for a moment as if frozen by the intensity of the attention everyone on hand was paying to the scene. Clint broke the spell himself by turning abruptly back toward the road and resuming his march in that direction with Jocelyn once again in tow.

Guffaws of derision exploded behind them. Several voices imitated the sound of a chicken cackling, but no one followed Clint and Jocelyn as they made their retreat from the flea market field and up the pathway to the roadside. Jocelyn felt her face redden as she scrambled to keep up. Her flush was partly anger for the way these people were treating a man she couldn't help siding with, but there was humiliation, as well. That part of her would have preferred that he launch himself into that bastion of musclebound creeps. She might even have pounced on them herself and helped Clint pound them as much as was possible before his inevitable defeat—and hers.

She had cast her glance away from him, struck by the irrationality of her own reaction. Otherwise, she might have missed the fleeting glimpse of a crouched figure on the opposite side of the road, vanishing into the underbrush so rapidly that she wondered whether she had actually seen anything at all.

Clint didn't give her much time to ponder that or anything else. They had reached the truck. He jerked the door open and hoisted her up onto the running board, then pushed her ahead of him into the cab and across the seat. Over the din of his slamming the door and jolting the engine to life, she could still hear the catcalls from the crowd they had left behind as he spun the truck in a tight U-turn and the gears ground angrily in preparation for roaring off down the road.

The bullet hit the windshield just as Clint's foot was about to hit the gas pedal.

Chapter Seven

The shot didn't come from the flea market side of the road. Jocelyn remembered the figure darting into the trees and believed she might know where the shot *had* come from. It ended up passing through the upper right-hand corner of the windshield just above her head, then out the open passenger-side window. It happened so fast that she barely registered the sound. In fact, for a moment she wasn't sure what had happened. The windshield was intact in front of her one instant, and the next there was a hole through the glass with a webbing of shatter lines around it.

She hadn't yet put her seat belt on when the bullet struck, and now there were other things on her mind. But when Clint tromped on the accelerator, she could have used the protection of that harness. She jolted forward toward the windshield as the truck leaped off the shoulder and left a line of wide tire marks in its wake. Jocelyn got her hands out in front of her just in time to catch the edge of the dashboard and keep herself from being propelled headlong into the glass.

"Buckle up," Clint barked. "And get your head down."

Jocelyn wasn't about to resent his gruff tone. Instead, she did what he said immediately, crouching down in the seat while yanking the heavy webbed belt around her and jamming the metal couplings together.

Meanwhile, Clint was driving the way the circumstances warranted—as if their lives could depend on it. He leaned forward over the steering wheel. Every ounce of determination and strength in his powerful body appeared to be trained on the road ahead, as if he might pull them along and out of danger by the mere force of his will to do so. His broad hands clutched the wheel hard enough to show the knuckle bones through his dark tanned skin. He glanced up at the rearview mirror periodically, but mostly his eyes were riveted on the road. Other than his command for her to buckle her seat belt, he gave no sign that he even remembered Jocelyn was with him.

They were traveling very fast. The highway was two lanes here, fairly wide with a soft, gravelly shoulder area on each side and a sunken drain-off ditch beyond that. The macadam had been patched and repatched many times over the years, as was so often the case with north country roads. The truck bounded in and out of depressions caused by winter freezing of the patched places and jounced over layers of blacktop repairs. Even with the belt to restrain her, Jocelyn was being tossed around quite violently. She grasped the dashboard with one hand and the window opening with the other to steady herself, while trying to keep her head out of the shooter's range at the same time.

"Damn," Clint cursed and wrenched the wheel once.

"What's the matter?" Jocelyn had been aware all along of how hard her heart was pounding. Now, it felt as if it was about to hammer itself out of her chest.

Clint jerked his head once in the direction of the rearview mirror. That was his only reply.

Jocelyn turned around and looked out the rear window. What she saw made her duck down out of sight. When she looked again it was only to peek furtively at the road behind them for a moment before pulling her head back in once more.

There was a truck behind them, one of the wide supercab rigs that were so popular up this way. A rack of headlamps ranged along the roof of the cab, and there was an extra-wide high-impact bumper on the front. Jocelyn had wondered on occasion what use these particular features might have, especially on a truck that was shined up and hand stenciled so elaborately that it seemed obvious the vehicle was never intended for real work. Right now, however, she could well imagine that custom bumper ramming into Clint's much lighter truck and shoving it along like a leaf caught up in a storm.

Jocelyn had the sensation of being chased by a machine gone wild. She would have liked to share that feeling with Clint rather than bear the burden of it on her own. However, he didn't look as if he was interested in communicating with anybody right now. In fact, with his lips curled back above the set of his jaw, he appeared just about as sinister and threatening as the souped-up truck barreling down the road after them.

Jocelyn glanced back through the rear window again to see the gap rapidly narrowing between pursuer and pursued. "He's gaining on us," she said.

"There's not much I can do about that. He's got a lot more horsepower going for him than we do."

"You think it's the same person who shot at us, don't you?"

"I think that's a strong possibility."

"Then what are we going to do when he catches up with us?"

Clint was obviously doing all he could at the moment. He had the accelerator pressed to the floorboard, and he was navigating the winding road with great skill at a high speed. Still, the black truck gained on them. There could be no doubt who would win the race, no matter how skilled a driver Clint might be.

"I'll do the best I can to keep us from getting our heads blown off," he said. "I think it's me he's after, but he might try to take you out, too. So, I want you to get down on the floor under the dashboard."

Jocelyn stared at him. She was recognizing for the first time the true desperateness of their situation.

"Do it now!" Clint shouted when she didn't move.

Jocelyn unlatched her safety belt. She slid onto the floor in front of the seat and wedged herself as best she could under the dashboard. From down there on the floor, she could feel every bump and pothole they hit reverberating straight up her spine. She cupped her hands over her head to keep it from making a painful tattoo against the underside of the dash. It occurred to her that she would absolutely hate to meet her final fate in such a ridiculous position.

"Get ready," Clint said, through gritted teeth. "Here he comes."

The roar of the other truck nearly drowned out his words. They had been overtaken. Now the black truck was pulling alongside them. Jocelyn couldn't resist straining to see as the black-glassed cab came into view through the window in Clint's door. He was sitting low in the seat, but there was no way he could pull himself entirely out of danger and still be able to see the road ahead.

"Hold on," he said. "I'm going to try to surprise him."

An evasive maneuver? Where could they go? There was a deep, rutted ditch to the right and trees beyond that. The demon truck was beside them now, blocking the leftward direction, and their engine power was not adequate to surge them ahead. What remained was taking the rear. That thought had come to Jocelyn as a kind of dark, half-hysterical joke. Suddenly, she realized it wasn't a joke at all. Suddenly, she knew what Clint was going to do.

He hit the brake just as she braced herself for the impact of an abrupt stop. The truck shuddered in response and lurched to a halt. Clint threw the shift into reverse and spun the wheel to bring the truck screeching around 180 degrees. He ground the gears into drive, tromped on the gas and they sped back down the road in the direction they had just come.

Jocelyn pulled herself out of her cramped refuge and onto the seat. She grabbed the seat back and peered out the rear window. The black truck was still clearly visible but receding ever farther into the distance. There had been time by now for that driver to realize what Clint had done and turn to pursue them once more. Instead, the black truck picked up speed and tore down the road away from them.

"He isn't following us!" Jocelyn exclaimed.

"No, he isn't," Clint said, as if pondering that. "What's going on?"

"Well, he could have given up on us because we're headed back where there are too many witnesses. Or maybe he just wanted to throw a scare into us, and he knows he did that. Or maybe he was just a good ol' boy driving like a maniac and making a little race out of it."

"Which do you think it is?" Jocelyn asked.

Clint slowed his truck down and pulled into a side road near the airfield and flea market.

"I haven't the slightest idea what's going on here. I don't know who shot at us. I don't know if it was the same guy in the truck. I don't even know who they're after, whether it's you or me. I just know there are questions to be asked, and I know where I'm going to start asking them."

He shoved the truck into gear, and they drove off down this new road that would neither take them past the shooting site nor back along the way the black truck had gone. Jocelyn wasn't sure where this road *would* take them. But since Clint might very well have saved her life just now, she was willing to follow his lead for the moment.

JOCELYN WASN'T KEPT in the dark for long about their destination. Clint didn't reduce speed much after their getaway. They zoomed along the back country roads, as if he might be trying to drive away his anger through bursts of acceleration. Then they made a turn, squealing onto a narrower and less trafficked road than the others. Jocelyn began to recognize landmarks. There was the cemetery with many of the stones fallen over, and the abandoned house with its roof stoved in.

"We're going to the Mapeses'," she said.

"Yes."

"What do you think we'll find out there?"

"I don't know," Clint replied. "But I don't trust the Mapes brothers. Just because Dolby acted friendly a while ago doesn't mean he's our friend. My observation of the Mapeses is that they're only friends to each other."

"I see," Jocelyn said, though she didn't see entirely. Northern New Yorkers could sometimes be characteristically close-minded. "I think we should try to remain open about this, Clint." She was trying to be diplomatic. "We have a lot of unanswered questions here, and we need to find out what is going on. It won't help if we let preconceived notions get in the way of discovering the truth."

Clint was silent for a moment, during which Jocelyn had the distinct impression he was trying to hog-tie his temper tightly enough to keep it from letting loose at her.

"Look, Jocelyn," he said finally. "I understand that you're trying to be fair and evenhanded about this. You don't want to fly off half-cocked, accusing people of taking potshots at us without evidence. The problem with that approach is we don't have any evidence. So, in the absence of evidence, we must fall back on instinct. That's what Patrick would say."

And Patrick ended up dead, would have been Jocelyn's reply, but she kept it to herself.

"My instincts," Clint concluded, "tell me the Mapes boys are in this somewhere, and not necessarily on our side of the fight."

"What fight? I didn't know we were in a fight."

Jocelyn looked up at Clint. She saw stubbornness in the expanse of his wide brow over unwavering eyes. She saw the determination and strength that had made it possible for him to walk away earlier from a fight against unbeatable odds and accept the ridicule that came with doing that. Sometimes it took a braver man to walk away. This morning Clint had proved himself that braver man.

She saw something else in his face, as well. She saw the shrewd intelligence needed to think up a way out when they were chased down by that monster truck. Such qualities in a person are not usually apparent so early in a relationship. Today had been a revealing day. For all its scariness, Jocelyn thanked the events of this morning for that.

But did she and Clint in fact have a relationship? Should she be thinking about him in those terms? Did he have any of the same thoughts about her?

Answers to those personal questions would have to wait. They had pulled into the gravel-and-dust parking area in front of the Mapes vegetable stand, which appeared to be closed. There would be other less intimate but equally crucial mysteries to investigate before this already eventful day was done.

"I'M GOING TO CHECK around the place," Clint said softly in Jocelyn's ear as she was about to step onto the porch.

She was glad of that because she had her own priorities to pursue here, and she intended to do so. She mustn't let herself lose sight of what she had set out to do today. She meant to dig and dig until she uncovered the truth about Philip and, along with it, the truth about the past five years of her life.

DeDe was wearing jeans today. Her hair was down and slightly disheveled, more the way it had been when she was chasing Philip's Lincoln down the road. A jean jacket had been tossed over one chair and sneakers and socks lay in a jumbled disarray in front of it. Obviously DeDe had come in just recently, for the jacket was too small for her brothers, at least the ones Jocelyn had met so far. And DeDe's feet were bare.

She was wearing dark red polish on her toenails, and it made her feet look pale and very feminine. Philip would have liked that, Jocelyn couldn't help thinking. Maybe she should have tried to do more things that Philip would have liked. A pang of regret jabbed her heart, but she had grown to know herself well enough over this past year to understand that the pang didn't come from having disappointed Philip. What Jocelyn regretted was that she hadn't really cared what Philip thought or felt about her. Given the discoveries of the past couple of days, she cared even less than before.

"Are you okay?" DeDe was asking. "You look a little flushed."

"Do I?"

Jocelyn touched her cheek with the back of her hand and felt the heat and dampness there. She touched her hair, as well. It was frizzing out into flyaway fullness, the way it did when the weather turned particularly humid. Or, during a wild ride at breakneck speed to escape flying bullets and a dreaded pursuer, she thought.

"I guess I must have been exerting myself more than usual this morning," she said, in a masterstroke of understatement.

DeDe didn't comment on that. She only nodded her head. Perhaps she was being courteous, not wanting to appear to be nosey.

Then again another possible explanation for DeDe's taciturn response occurred to Jocelyn. Maybe DeDe wasn't more curious about Jocelyn's disarrayed appearance because DeDe already knew its cause. Maybe Clint was right about the Mapeses' being mixed up in this morning's events. Maybe DeDe was even the specific Mapes in the mix.

Jocelyn glanced once more from DeDe's bare feet to the discarded footwear on the floor. Maybe DeDe wasn't as resigned to her former rival's presence as she appeared to be yesterday. Maybe she harbored a resentment deep enough to be motivation for an act of revenge. Maybe that bullet hadn't been meant for Clint, after all.

"Why don't you sit down," DeDe was saying. "You really don't look too good to me."

DeDe took Jocelyn's arm and urged her toward a chair. She didn't resist. Whether DeDe had been her assailant earlier or not, she certainly had made a salient point just now. Jocelyn definitely needed to sit down. She had made the mistake of slowing down just long enough for the stress of this tension-packed morning to catch up with her. That impact swept through her like a wave, leaving her suddenly more shaky on her feet than she liked to be. She followed DeDe's lead and sat down.

"Is there anything I can get you?" DeDe actually sounded concerned.

"This may sound like a strange request, but would you mind if I took my boots and socks off? I think I've developed a nasty blister on my heel."

"That doesn't sound strange at all," DeDe said with a smile. "You probably noticed I go barefoot a lot myself around here. No reason why you shouldn't do the same."

"Thanks," Jocelyn said, and busied herself with pulling off her boots while DeDe hurried out of the room.

Maybe DeDe's present helpfulness was a pretense meant to disguise some very unfriendly intentions, but Jocelyn couldn't help hoping that wasn't the case. She couldn't help liking DeDe Mapes, no matter how strongly the circumstances reminded Jocelyn that they had been adversaries in the past and might very well be adversaries still.

Was it really rational to feel positively about the woman who had been her husband's lover? Rational or not, those feelings persisted as DeDe hurried back in with a number of first-aid items on a tray.

"Let's take a look at that heel," she said.

Jocelyn had removed her boots and socks. She might have insisted on ministering to herself, except that she recognized what she suspected to be DeDe's take-charge persona, the one she most likely used to keep brothers like Davis and Dolby in line. She set the first-aid tray on a small wooden table next to Jocelyn's chair.

"You've got a blister, all right," DeDe said, lifting Jocelyn's right foot and inspecting the damage her scrunched-up sock had done. "Whatever possessed you to keep walking around like that? It must have been hurting you real bad."

Jocelyn couldn't see DeDe's face well enough, bent over her work as she was, to search for signs of insincerity. "I had other things on my mind," Jocelyn said.

"You must have to let yourself work up a humdinger like this one."

Jocelyn listened carefully to those words, trying to detect any deceit in their tone. She heard nothing like that. Of course, Clint had said the Mapeses weren't to be trusted. Maybe he was right and DeDe was crafty enough to keep that craftiness from showing. After all, she had been duplicitous enough to carry on an affair with a married man. But DeDe claimed not to know "Reggie" was married until late in the game. In that case, Philip had been the truly duplicitous one. Jocelyn's head was on the verge of spinning from the confusing entanglement of possible betrayals here. There was simply no way to know who could and could not be trusted.

"I have my own remedy for blisters, especially for big ones like this. It works like a charm," DeDe went on. "But you'll have to put your trust in me that I know what I'm doing."

Trust! A danger warning rang loud and clear for Jocelyn. She had just been thinking about that very same, very touchy subject.

"What exactly are you planning to do?" she asked, making no attempt to hide her skepticism.

DeDe's next move did little to calm those doubts. She had picked up a long sewing needle from the tray. She lit a wooden match by striking the head against the rough fieldstone of the fireplace, then aimed the point of the needle into the flame. When the point turned blue and then dark, DeDe shook the match till the flame went out. She gripped the needle carefully, not letting the sterilized point come into contact with anything.

"This is really my mother's remedy," DeDe said as she was performing the sterilization. "It probably was her mother's before her and so on back through the generations. My family's got more cures and treatments than you can count. They've all been passed on down the line that way. You may have noticed some of my herbs growing along the side of the house. I've got more out back, too. You most likely smelled them even if you didn't see them. You'd be surprised what some of that stuff can take care of. Being from the city and all, you might not put much store by what we call hill medicine. But I can tell you, I've seen it work more times than not. I'll put my hand to heaven on that."

DeDe actually did lift her hand heavenward for an instant. Jocelyn could recall the strong fragrance of what could have been herbs while she was sitting on the Mapes porch yesterday. As for home remedies, she did believe they could be effective. In fact, that was one of the few areas in which she had positive experiences with her mother and her mother's friends. Their hippy cures had worked more often than not, just as DeDe said about her family prescriptives. Besides, Jocelyn's heel was beginning to feel very tender, indeed.

"You're going to lance it. Right?" Jocelyn asked.

"That's a fancy way of saying that I'm going to puncture the blister and let the fluid out."

Jocelyn nodded. "What will you do after that?"

"Then I put on a special mixture that will dry the blister up all the way and keep it dry."

"One of your herbal mixtures?"

DeDe laughed. "Nothing that exotic. Not for the likes of a blister, even a monster one like this." She pointed to a plastic bottle of rubbing alcohol on the tray. "This stuff is cheap to buy and doesn't cost me any work, either. Most important, it does the trick. I believe in the old-fashioned hill ways, but I believe in common sense, too. But if you don't want me messing around with your foot, that's fine with me. It's your blister, not mine."

"No, no. I didn't say that," Jocelyn hastened to make clear. Concentrating so much attention on her heel seemed to have made it hurt all the worse. Pain had begun to take precedence over any qualms she might have about DeDe. "I'm sure you know what you're doing."

DeDe leaned back on her heels from her position over Jocelyn's foot and looked her hard in the face for a moment. "I get it," she said. "You think that because of what went on between Reggie and me, maybe you shouldn't put much trust in me." DeDe paused and continued studying Jocelyn for another moment. "I can certainly understand why you might be inclined to come up with a notion like that."

For a split second only, Jocelyn considered evading DeDe's very accurate observation. Then she decided to confront it straight on.

"You're right," she said. "That is exactly what I was thinking."

DeDe nodded and began to hoist herself up from her squatting position. Jocelyn reached out and took DeDe's arm to stop her rise.

"But what I'm thinking now is that my heel really hurts and what you say you want to do sounds like it could help. So I would be very grateful if you would just go ahead and do it."

DeDe hesitated a moment, then nodded again. "I'll do that," she said, and got down on her haunches once more to set to work.

BY THE TIME Clint appeared on the other side of the screen door, DeDe had finished her doctoring. She was still cradling Jocelyn's ankle in her hand and patting the last piece of tape into place along the soft bandage she had made. Looking from Clint to DeDe, Jocelyn found it difficult to determine which of them looked more surprised.

"What are you doing here?" DeDe demanded. Whatever gentleness had come over her during her role as nurse to Jocelyn had disappeared.

"I'm with Mrs. Wald," Clint said, nodding toward Jocelyn.

His tone was none too friendly, either. Jocelyn wondered if he might have referred to her by her married name because the reminder of Philip would be upsetting to DeDe. Meanwhile, DeDe was looking back and forth between Clint and Jocelyn as if trying to assimilate the shock of learning that they were together.

"Then I guess you had better come on in," DeDe finally said to Clint without looking at him.

"Actually, I think we should be leaving now," Jocelyn said, putting her foot down on the floor and testing a bit of weight on it. She was amazed by how little discomfort she now felt.

"Didn't you stop by because you wanted to ask me something?" DeDe asked.

Clint held his ground outside the screen door.

"You're right. I did," Jocelyn said. "But my questions can wait."

If Clint hadn't shown up, Jocelyn might have stayed around and talked with DeDe more. But the man obviously made DeDe uncomfortable; Jocelyn didn't think that was any way to repay a kindness. Besides, one of the things Jocelyn wanted to ask about was the reason for that discomfort. She couldn't do that in front of Clint.

"Wait a minute," DeDe said. "I want to give you something before you go." She hurried out of the room.

"What's been going on here, anyway?" Clint asked in a loud whisper through the screen.

Jocelyn signaled for him to be quiet. He sighed and turned away from the doorway, only to pace from the edge of the porch and back.

A few moments later, DeDe returned. She was carrying a pair of plastic-thonged sandals in one hand and a folded piece of paper in the other.

"These should fit you," she said, putting the sandals down at Jocelyn's feet. "And these should help you answer some of those questions of yours."

She pressed the folded paper into Jocelyn's hand. She could feel something hard through the folds. After opening it she looked back up at DeDe but did not smile. Smiling would not have been appropriate, though Jocelyn was tempted to give DeDe a hug all the same.

Instead, Jocelyn just said, "Thanks," and stuffed the paper and its contents into her pocket. She said, "Thanks for these, too," and shoved her feet into the thongs. "I'll bring them back tomorrow."

"Don't you worry about that. They're yours," DeDe said. "But that doesn't mean you can't come back tomorrow if you have a mind to."

"Good," Jocelyn said, and she did smile this time.

She and Clint left the house and walked to the top of the path that led down to the parking lot. Jocelyn was limping only slightly but needed some help down the hill. Clint took a firm grip on her arm. He also took advantage of the opportunity to lean toward her with a hushed question.

"What were the two of you up to back there?"

"DeDe nursed my blister back to health, and then she gave me a present."

"You mean the sandals?" Clint was carrying Jocelyn's rain boots with her socks stuffed into them.

"No," she said. "I mean this." She pulled the folded paper just far enough from her pocket for Clint to get a peek.

"What's that?" he asked.

"*That* is the key to Philip's house in the woods and a map for getting there."

Chapter Eight

"Don't you think you've had enough for one day?" Clint asked when Jocelyn insisted on going to the house in the woods that afternoon.

"Actually, I think I've had more than enough for several days, but that doesn't mean I'm going to get off this train before the end of the line."

They were back in Clint's truck now and headed away from the Mapes property.

"Did you find out anything from looking around at the Mapeses'?" Jocelyn asked.

"It's what I didn't find that's most interesting."

"Then what didn't you find?"

"There's no black truck with black glass anywhere around that house. At least, there isn't one now."

Jocelyn came close to breathing a sigh of relief. She really didn't want DeDe to be mixed up in anything that might mean trouble for her. Philip had given her enough to be troubled about already. Jocelyn didn't feel responsible for that trouble in any way, but she did feel a kind of kinship with DeDe because of it. Philip had also given Jocelyn a good deal to be troubled about. She and DeDe had that in common.

"However," Clint broke in on Jocelyn's reverie of relief, "that doesn't mean the truck wasn't at Mapeses' earlier and somebody drove it away in between. Maybe one of the brothers is out there tooling around the countryside right now, laughing it up about how he almost shot us in the head and ran us off the road."

Jocelyn did sigh this time, but in exasperation, not relief. "Yes, I suppose that is a possibility, the way all worst-case scenarios are possible."

"Look, Jocelyn. Do you want to find out the truth whatever it may be? Or do you want to find out the truth as long as it's what you want to hear?"

Jocelyn spun around toward him with such abruptness that she even startled herself. "I don't think that is at all fair," she snapped. "I've faced enough unwelcome truth in the past twenty-four hours to prove my stamina in that department several times over."

"You're right about that," Clint said more softly. "And that is exactly why I would like to take you back to your trailer now while I have a look around that house of your husband's. I don't think you need to put yourself through that yet. I can report what's there to you. I'll even take pictures, if you like."

Jocelyn's flash of anger was no match for the concern in his eyes or the plaintive expression on his face. Still, she knew what she had to do. She touched his arm and leaned toward him, both to get his attention and to let him know how determined she was.

"I appreciate your kindness. I appreciate everything you've done for me today. But I am going out to that house this afternoon, and I want to be driving my own car when I do it. So, please take me back to Tranquility."

Clint opened his mouth to protest. Before he could speak, she gripped his arm tighter and said, "Please, do that for me now," with unmistakable emphasis in her voice.

Clint clamped his mouth shut and nodded once. She could tell he wasn't happy about acquiescing, but he hadn't had much choice. For a woman who hadn't asserted herself much in the past six years, Jocelyn wasn't doing badly at it. After all Clint Conti was no pushover.

In fact, she told herself, if he were a pushover, the two of them might have been shot in the heads and run off the road just as he was saying a moment ago.

The prospect made her shudder. She turned toward the passenger window and away from Clint so he wouldn't see how upset she got just thinking about this traumatic day. She didn't want him to become even more protective.

Jocelyn stared out of the window, barely seeing the roadside move past. She was thinking over the morning—the airfield revelations, the challenge to Clint at the flea market, the shot through the windshield, the terrifying truck chase—and then the afternoon and her visit with DeDe. Once upon a time, maybe just the day before yesterday, Jocelyn would have struggled to make sense of these occurrences. She didn't do that now. Something she had learned very recently told her that everything doesn't necessarily make sense no matter how much you may want it to.

Jocelyn accepted that, though she didn't feel exactly good about it. What she did feel good about was her capacity for accepting it, without Philip or Clint or anybody else sugarcoating it for her. Only a trace of nostalgia remained for the time when unpleasant burdens had been borne by someone other than herself.

Still, she was relieved that Clint didn't strike up another conversation on the way back to her campsite. She might feel stronger now, but she didn't feel like dwelling on her troubles at the moment.

STRONGER AND NEWLY assertive or not, Jocelyn wasn't able to talk down one argument of Clint's for accompanying her to the house Philip and DeDe had shared. The directions on DeDe's map were fairly complicated, and Clint knew the area better than Jocelyn did. She would have been foolish to risk getting lost in the back country where many of the roads are poorly marked or not marked at all. It made much more sense to have Clint lead the way in his truck while Jocelyn followed in the Lincoln.

There were other reasons for having Clint along in addition to his pathfinder abilities. First of all, she was dreading this visit to Philip's hideaway. It would be better to have someone along with her, especially a friend. Clint was, amazingly enough, the closest thing she had to a friend in this part of the country right now.

They stopped outside of Lowville to gas up so they'd be certain not to run out of fuel on the trip into the woods. She watched as Clint pumped gas into his truck. Even the simple task revealed the power of his muscular body. Yet he kept that power under control and didn't find it necessary to flaunt it.

She could not deny, and didn't even want to deny at the moment, that she found him very attractive. During this period of relative calm, she could admit to herself how much she enjoyed watching him move. The parts of his tall, wide body worked together with a grace that was both fluid and masculine.

She also liked to watch his hands, the way he grasped things quickly and deftly, as if he knew exactly what he wanted and why and would be able to hold on to it once he found it. She knew she would like those hands to hold her. She even knew she would like to have those hands touching her body. That knowledge was disturbing to her, almost as disturbing as the awareness that she had never reveled in watching Philip move or taken pleasure in seeing his hands and imagining what they could do to her.

Jocelyn couldn't help being distracted by such thoughts. On her way to her late husband's secret love nest, she felt little anxiety or anger. Instead she was experiencing a sense of elation that she knew came from being in the company of a man who made her very aware that she was a woman. That awareness made her feel more alive than she could remember feeling for a long, long time. She felt only marginally guilty that she hadn't felt this way until after her husband was dead.

After leaving the gas station and the main highway, Jocelyn maneuvered the Lincoln along roads that led deep into the woods. The wide car took up most of the passageway down an avenue of trees and foliage. The air was sweet with summer leaf scent sharpened by the occasional strong presence of pine. Back from the road, where the trees grew dense and close together, the forest floor looked dark, cool and inviting. She could imagine herself reclining there for a lazy afternoon nap. She could also imagine Clint there with her. She didn't discourage that fantasy. She understood that these feelings of hers were simply a part of waking from the long emotional sleep of widowhood and the even longer lethargy of a marriage without passion.

Philip's house turned out to be an unpleasant reminder of other shortcomings in her marriage. The house itself was not what she would have chosen for herself. It was much too suburban for her taste and seemed out of place among the clusters of pine, birch and maple. The white siding and one-story ranch layout would have been much more at home behind a manicured lawn and some very tame shrubs than out here in the wilderness, besieged by leaf-clogged gutters and the perils of pine pitch.

"It looks like the kind of house Philip would choose," Jocelyn said to Clint after they had parked the vehicles and met on the walk leading to the front stoop.

"In what way?" Clint asked.

Jocelyn looked the place over once again. "Aluminum siding for low maintenance. No-nonsense design. Not particularly imaginative, but orderly and under control."

"Was Philip like that? Orderly and under control?"

"Very much so," Jocelyn said with a certain sadness in her voice and walked ahead up the path.

She had to rattle the key in the lock several times before it would turn. Maybe nobody had been here for a while. Her first step inside told her that wasn't true. Everything was neat and clean with no sign of dust or disuse anywhere. There were even healthy, blooming plants on the windowsills and more suspended from the ceiling by woven hangings. Jocelyn recognized some of the same floral varieties she had seen at the Mapes house. In fact, evidence of DeDe's colorful, relaxed taste was everywhere. The exterior and general architecture of this house might have been Philip's choice, but the interior definitely belonged to DeDe, who had made it her own.

Jocelyn hadn't really put herself into the Genessee Street house. She had gone along with Philip's preferences for the most part. That was how they ended up with some things she didn't really care for, like the leather couches in the living room and the standing potted fern between them. She had always thought they made the place look more like the waiting area of a dentist's office than a room where a family might gather. Here, in the warm home DeDe had created, Jocelyn wished she had asserted more of her own choices into her life with Philip, and not only in matters of interior decorating.

"Are you all right?"

Clint's question was gentle and solicitous. He was watching her with concern in his eyes. Jocelyn was touched by that.

"I'm fine," she said.

She smiled and touched his arm to reassure him that she spoke the truth. He covered her hand with his before she could take it away.

"I don't imagine this is too easy for you," he said.

"Actually, it isn't as hard as I expected it would be."

He nodded but looked as if he didn't quite understand what she was saying. He also didn't let go of her hand.

"My husband and I weren't really very close," she said quietly. "If he hadn't died, we probably wouldn't have stayed together."

"I didn't know that," Clint said.

"I barely knew it myself at the time."

"What about your husband? Did he know you were thinking about leaving him?"

Jocelyn sighed. "No, he didn't." She gestured around the room. "Obviously, he wouldn't have been too brokenhearted if he had known."

Clint squeezed her hand before letting it go. "I don't make a practice of speaking ill of the dead," he said. "But anyone who wouldn't be brokenhearted to lose you mustn't have been a very wise man."

"I certainly wasn't very smart myself when it came to knowing what was going on right under my nose."

Clint shrugged. "We all tend to trust what we've been told by the people close to us. We don't want to think that they might be deceiving us."

A sudden deepening of his voice made Jocelyn suspect he could be speaking personally, about something in his own life that might be troubling him. He turned away from her, and she didn't press him further.

"Why don't you take a look around," he said. "I imagine you might want to do that on your own. I'll just wait for you here."

"Okay."

Jocelyn appreciated Clint's sensitivity. For a big man, he certainly was graceful...and not just in the way he moved. Her heart went out to him and whatever trouble it was she had sensed in the seriousness of his tone a few moments ago.

Clint remained in the living room as Jocelyn walked through the rest of the house. She wasn't sure what she had expected to find, but she didn't feel comfortable about searching too diligently for whatever it might be. She felt like a trespasser in somebody else's private territory, almost as if Philip and DeDe had been the married couple and Jocelyn was the other woman.

She saw clothes she recognized as Philip's hanging in the master bedroom closet and marveled that she hadn't paid enough attention to his wardrobe to notice these things missing from the bundle she packed up and sent to a homeless shelter after his death. She had anticipated a renewal of her anger and her feelings of betrayal when she saw firsthand the actual evidence of Philip's life with DeDe. What Jocelyn felt instead was sadness for three misdirected lives. She might not have been in love with Philip, but she had liked him most of the time. She wished he had been able to spend more of his final months here in this place, where she suspected he had found a more satisfying life than the one he had with her—or the one she had with him.

Philip had married her because she fulfilled a need in him to be in charge. He had acted more as her father than her husband. Then, when he tired of that, he found a lover. And when Jocelyn outgrew her need for his control and protection, he was not around to recognize it. Maybe they could have had a different relationship if Philip had been interested in allowing that change to happen. Then again, maybe there wasn't enough basis of feeling between them to build a real marriage on.

The drawer of the nightstand was slightly ajar. She grabbed the knob and pulled it open. She felt she had the right to do that for some reason, as if the life that had been carried on in this house had been lived at her expense and she was entitled to some redress. The mundane contents of the drawer made her feel suddenly silly. There was a bottle of aspirin and a copy of a romance novel that DeDe must have been reading. A few hairpins were scattered in the bottom of the drawer next to an empty notepad and a pencil.

Jocelyn was about to close the drawer when she noticed the yellow package just behind the romance novel. Jocelyn recognized it as a bag from a film-processing company, the kind they use for finished photographs. She pulled the drawer open a few inches farther. The bag had been opened, but there were still photos inside. Jocelyn rubbed her hand on her jeans, trying to decide what to do. Almost automatically her hand reached out and took the yellow envelope from the drawer.

She guessed that the photos must have been taken by DeDe. They were mostly nature scenes. Several shots were closeups of wild flowers. She had an eye for color and gentle beauty. There were a few landscape shots of fields with high, blue skies above them, a clearing at the edge of a wood. Jocelyn didn't recognize the locations exactly, but they looked like north country scenes. They were well-composed photographs, and that convinced Jocelyn that Philip couldn't have taken them. He had no talent with a camera and would cut off heads or other significant aspects of whatever he was trying to shoot.

The few photos of people in this batch had the heads all intact. They had obviously been taken on the same day. Jocelyn did recognize this location. They had been taken at the airport. Part of the hangar was visible in the background. Philip's plane was in front of it. The sight of the vehicle that had taken her husband to his death brought a tear to Jocelyn's eye.

Philip was in the picture, too, looking casual and relaxed. There were people standing behind him, most likely regulars at the airport. Jocelyn didn't recognize any of them. Altogether there were three photos from the airport. They had probably been taken in rapid succession because the same people were in each of them. Jocelyn guessed that DeDe had been trying to capture just the right smile on Philip's face. In one of them she appeared to have done that. He was looking into the camera with an affectionate grin that made Jocelyn's heart lurch. She was sure he must have looked at her that way at some point in their relationship, but right now she couldn't remember when.

She returned that shot of Philip smiling to the envelope and took one of the other three. She slid the photo into a pocket of the jacket she still wore tied around her waist. She had no idea what she would do with the picture, but having it made her feel she had conducted the investigation she had come here for and now she could leave. She replaced the envelope exactly as she had found it in the bedside table drawer and left the room.

Now Jocelyn was eager to get out of the house. Clint watched as she slammed the door behind her and began rattling the key in the lock trying to get it to turn. Her impatience only aggravated the problem. She pulled the key out to insert it the other way around and this time couldn't get it to fit into the keyhole at all.

"Let me help you with that," Clint said.

Jocelyn rattled the key twice more before yielding to Clint with a grimace. He maneuvered the key a few times more with no more luck than she had.

"I've got a can of WD-40 in the glove compartment of the truck," he said. "Could you get it for me?"

Jocelyn hurried down the walk to the truck and yanked open the door on the driver's side. She leaned across the steering wheel and punched the button on the glove box hoping she would recognize WD-whatever when she saw it. A bundle of maps had to be pulled out first. Behind them was an odd assortment of keys, a pair of pliers and a blue can of what Jocelyn was looking for. She pulled out the can and was stuffing the maps back into the compartment when she noticed that two smaller things had fallen onto the truck floor.

She picked up a folded paper that looked like registration papers for the truck. The second item was more interesting, and Jocelyn couldn't resist looking. It was a photograph, not like the color shot she had found in the house, but older and black and white. Two young men grinned at her with arms around each other's necks. They were both shirtless in an obviously summer setting. Clint was younger, though still very recognizable. His hair was shorter, but that wasn't what riveted her attention.

She had, of course, already noticed the broadness of his chest in person. Thus, the picture shouldn't have come as a surprise, but it did. Even in black and white, she could see the tawniness of his tan beneath a thatch of dark, curling hair. The musculature was already well defined, though he must have been only in his mid-twenties here. His shoulders were wide and hard above a chiseled collar bone, and Jocelyn's breath caught in her throat at the bulge of his biceps. She touched the expanse of his chest with her forefinger, as if she might have been able to feel the hard flesh there.

The photograph was creased, and its corners had crumpled with age. Jocelyn brought the glossy surface closer to her face in order to see Clint more clearly. It was then that she noticed the faded pencil marks above the heads of the two figures in the picture. Actually, only the indentations made by the pencil point were still visible. She made out "Clint" next to his smiling face. The other figure was labelled "Patrick."

Sadness touched Jocelyn's heart as she looked at the two brothers smiling together, so obviously enjoying each other's company. This was the brother that Clint had lost. She searched Patrick's face for some resemblance to his brother and found it in the breadth of his forehead and the angle of his chin. He was smaller than Clint, but the family relationship was evident.

Something else was evident from this picture, but it took a moment for Jocelyn to register it because the recognition was so unexpected. She had seen Patrick's face or one very much like it before. She stopped to think about exactly where. She knew it was recent, but how could that be? Clint had said his brother died last year.

Jocelyn gasped. Now she knew where she had seen that face before, but it hardly seemed possible. She reached into the pocket of her jacket and drew out another photograph, the one she had found in the nightstand. Jocelyn stared at the color photo and then at the black-and-white one. She looked back and forth between them twice more. She had little difficulty verifying what she saw there. The implications of that discovery were not as easy to comprehend.

He was older in the color photo, bigger physically than in the black and white. He had also grown a stubble on his chin, and his hair had a darker tint. Still, there could be no question that the young man in both photographs, standing just behind Philip in one and arm around Clint in the other, was one and the same person. The young man in both pictures was Patrick Conti.

Chapter Nine

Jocelyn slipped the photograph back into the glove compartment, on the bottom underneath the maps so Clint wouldn't be likely to know she had seen it. The color photo was still in her hand. She stared at the troubling face in that picture, the two troubling faces, counting Philip's.

Patrick Conti had known her late husband. There was no date on the back of the photo, but the shirt Philip had on was one he wore a lot last summer. Both men were smiling, though not directly at each other. They appeared to be at ease together. What could their relationship have been? Jocelyn had never heard Philip speak of anyone named Patrick, but Philip had never talked much to her about his associates, especially not those he did business with. What business could he have had with Patrick Conti? Most likely they were passing acquaintances from the airfield. But then why were they having their picture taken together? And why were they smiling in that self-satisfied way? These were perplexing questions, but not the most perplexing raised for Jocelyn by her discovery of the two photographs.

Did Clint know that his brother was acquainted with her husband? Her instincts told her he did and that this was a significant piece of knowledge for him. That's why he had the photograph close at hand in his glove compartment. But what was that significance, and why hadn't he told her about it? She'd wondered why Clint had taken such an interest in her investigation of Philip's Lewis County past. Now she had a feeling, stronger even than instinct, that Clint was a part of that past somehow. Even if Jocelyn believed in coincidences, she wouldn't believe that this photo was one.

Jocelyn stuffed the color photograph back into her jacket pocket. She would have liked to tell herself she was being paranoid, imagining things, making mountains out of molehills. Everybody in the north country knew everybody else. That's how it was in a small, close-knit rural community. Philip could have been acquainted with a lot of people around here. Or was it Reggie Williams they knew?

And who was Clint Conti really? She knew almost nothing about him. Yet, she had shared with him the agonizing experiences of the past few days. She had even entertained lustful thoughts of him. Now, she suspected that she had made a terrible mistake. So much deception! Her head rang with it.

"Did you find it?" Clint called from the stoop.

I found it, all right, Jocelyn almost snapped, even though he wasn't talking about the photograph from the glove compartment. She grabbed the blue can from the seat and climbed out of the truck. She wasn't exactly sure what she should do next, at least not about Clint. So, for now she would do nothing, except take him this stuff he needed for the keyhole, and get out of here as fast as she could—and by herself.

THE EXCUSES Jocelyn used to get away from Clint sounded flimsy even to her until she resorted to playing for sympathy.

"Seeing this house has affected me more than I thought it would," she had said. "I need to be alone now."

That was all very true, of course, but not for the reasons he would assume. He would think that the reminders of Philip's betrayal had been too much for her to take. Thoughts of betrayal were in fact haunting her heart as she bounced the big Lincoln over the winding road through the woods in the deepening twilight. Evening was coming on, and the denseness of the forest was bringing the dark down fast.

Jocelyn remembered imagining herself among the trees with Clint, locked in an embrace on a bed of pine needles. That memory upset her so much that she jerked the steering wheel too drastically to the right and veered into what little there was of a shoulder on the narrow road. She was so close to plowing straight into the trees that underbrush and branches scraped the right side of the car. There would be marks on the sleek, hand-rubbed finish Philip had cared so much about.

Jocelyn jerked the wheel to the left, deliberately and with considerable anger this time. Right now, Jocelyn wouldn't mind if she had made a dent in Philip's precious car the size of one of these tree trunks. She had decided, almost without thinking about it, that she was going to get rid of this hulking vehicle, anyway. It was too much like the other remnants of her marriage to Philip—cumbersome, out of sync with her present needs and kept around too long after they should have been left behind as part of a life now past and done with.

The Lincoln burst out of the trees onto the highway, and Jocelyn gunned the big engine down the road. One thing this monster car was good for was making a fast getaway. She sped along the rural route, half expecting the wail of a state trooper's siren to come sweeping after her out of one of those cornfield crannies. That's where Smokey would sometimes lie in wait for country boys with hot pickup trucks, barreling down the blacktop at speeds imprudent for conditions, as the law books called it.

Jocelyn cracked a rueful smile. Ever since she arrived in Lewis County this summer, she had been conducting her life at a speed imprudent for conditions. The dominant impression in her mind was that Clint Conti was the catalyst that had catapulted her onto this breakneck course. That might not be a totally accurate evaluation of the events of these past days, at least not on the surface of things. He hadn't been the one who brought her illusions about her marriage crashing down around her. He hadn't been the one taking potshots at them from the roadside.

Nonetheless, Clint hadn't told her the whole truth. She was all but absolutely certain of that. Or maybe she just needed a scapegoat to vent her anger on. Clint Conti was the perfect candidate for that role as far as she was concerned. She pushed the accelerator even closer to the floor and felt her fury rage with the roar of the engine.

If Conti had appeared in front of her on the highway just then, she could easily imagine herself running him down, striking him full force with this oversized gas hog, smack up against the chrome grillwork Philip kept polished more perfectly than a dowager keeps her silver. That would take care of both of them in one big bang—these two men who had used her less well than she deserved. Jocelyn tore down the road as if she might outrun the past, and maybe even the present, if she could only get enough speed out of this crate to do so.

SHE REACHED Tranquility campground at just about suppertime. The pool area was quiet, the children having been drawn back to their campsites by the gnawing of hungry, young bellies. Pleasant aromas of barbecue grilling reminded Jocelyn that she hadn't eaten since breakfast. She was surprised to hear her own stomach rumble in response. The emotional upheaval of this hectic day might have banished all attraction for food. Jocelyn marveled at the way the body keeps chugging along with the business of keeping a person alive even when the psyche is frozen in shock somewhere back down the road.

Across the road from Jocelyn's campsite, Sonny Shannon had set his small hibachi on the wooden picnic table in front of his trailer. No cloth covered the rough board surface of the table that came with the campsite. A bottle of catsup, a box of salt and a package of paper plates were the only amenities Sonny had provided himself in his Spartan, bachelor spread. He did have a healthy fire going. In fact, flames leaped through the hibachi grate and well above it, almost high enough to endanger the still-sagging awning of his RV.

Jocelyn bit her lip to keep from laughing at what had to be the most inept attempt at outdoor living that she had ever witnessed. She smelled the burned meat even before she got close enough to see the blackened remains of four wieners still partly aflame on top of the hibachi grate.

"You're supposed to let the flames die down before you put the food on," she said. "The coals are actually hottest when they aren't red anymore."

"Is that right?"

Sonny nodded as if he might be pondering the mysteries of charcoal as he poked at the shriveled carcasses of his hot dogs with a pair of long-handled barbecue tongs. He was still wearing his sweatshirt and jeans. Sometime during the day, he had cut the sleeves short on the former. Nonetheless, his forehead glistened from standing so near this very hot blaze.

"I think I have come up with the secret of keeping myself from starving on a camping trip," he said.

"And would you mind sharing that secret with me?" After the trials of her day, Sonny's much less traumatic dilemmas couldn't help but strike her as funny.

"I wouldn't mind at all. You can feel free to publish it, as a matter of fact. The secret is to keep lots of peanut butter and jelly on hand."

Jocelyn laughed. "That's true. You always need a backup plan when you're out here in the wilderness."

"If the weather don't get you, the charcoal will." Sonny used the tongs to pick up the unappetizing wieners. "It's time to put these dogs out of their misery," he said as he dropped them into a brown paper supermarket bag on the ground near the table. "I guess it's going to be P.B. and J. for me tonight, after all."

"Do you happen to have some more of those around?" Jocelyn gestured toward the charred remains in the paper bag. "Ones not as yet incinerated, that is?"

"Sure," Sonny said. "I even got rolls and mustard and relish. The dining room at the Ritz ain't got nothing on me."

"Why don't you let me see what I can salvage of your supper," Jocelyn said. "I've had a lot of experience with this kind of thing."

"It's all yours," Sonny said, presenting the barbecue tongs to her with a flourish. "Consider me your unable assistant, ready to fetch, carry and stumble over my own feet on demand."

Jocelyn chuckled. He certainly was a jovial person when he chose to be. She remembered her first sight of him, pitching a tantrum over the awning, and wondered if she might have missed a similar loss of control over the fire earlier or prevented one from happening with her arrival on the scene.

"I have to tell you I appreciate your helping me out," he was saying. "I'm a fish out of water when it comes to this roughing-it stuff. A good neighbor is something I could really use right now."

Jocelyn nodded as she employed the tongs to begin removing excess charcoal from the hibachi where Sonny had dumped at least three times as many briquettes as he needed for such a small grill. She focused extra hard on what she was doing so she wouldn't have to look him in the eye. She knew she hadn't come here to be a good neighbor, and she wasn't exactly proud of using that ruse to accomplish what she actually had come for.

JOCELYN DISGUISED her true agenda until supper had been cooked and served. Sonny had produced a can of baked beans and a bag of potato chips from the trailer and had insisted she eat with him. Jocelyn was not about to refuse, and not just because of all the questions she had for him, either. She was so hungry that she felt like devouring the hot dogs raw and spooning mouthfuls of beans straight from the can. The meal might not be the most nutritious she had ever eaten, but it certainly was among the most welcome.

When Jocelyn asked Sonny if he had a table covering of some kind, he disappeared into the trailer, then reemerged with a large unopened package of cotton dish towels.

"I saw these in the supermarket when I was buying the hot dogs," he said. "I thought they might come in handy. I'm not quite sure for what, though."

Jocelyn refrained from remarking that a dozen dish towels was probably more than he needed on a pretty basic campsite, especially considering all of the other more essential items he was so obviously missing. She spread out the towels lengthwise to make a serviceable overlapping tablecloth beneath the paper plates and condiment bottles. Jocelyn made certain Sonny put a piece of wood under the Coleman lantern instead of setting it directly on the cloth-covered surface. He had almost started one fire already tonight with the hibachi and the awning. She would prefer that he didn't set the table ablaze for his next act as a man of the wilderness. She had begun to feel a bit protective of this babe in the woods who must be at least thirty years old.

Still, she hadn't forgotten her real reason for coming over here tonight. She waited for the opening she needed. She didn't want to be too obvious about it. That opening came just after Sonny offered her a can of beer and she had accepted. He popped the ring top and handed her the can. If he had a glass in the trailer, he didn't think to offer that, as well. Still, the cold liquid felt very good on her throat. She was glad that whatever else Sonny might have failed to bring along on this camping trip, he had not forgotten the well-iced cooler chest.

"I noticed you weren't around much today," Sonny said after they had both eaten enough to assuage the initial ravenous stage of hunger. "Were you out taking in the sights?"

There it was—the opening she had been waiting for. She was careful not to leap at it too eagerly.

"A friend of the Delaneys took me to meet some acquaintances of my late husband's that I hadn't known before," she said.

"What friend of the Delaneys would that be?"

He had pried the opening even wider for her by asking that. Jocelyn was careful to maintain her loose, casual tone.

"His name is Clint Conti. I think you might know him."

"What makes you think that?" Sonny asked.

"He told me that you were on the police force with his brother."

"That's right," Sonny said. "His brother Patrick and I used to work together. Clint and I used to play sports against each other in high school, too. Did he tell you that?"

"He may have mentioned it."

Jocelyn picked up her fork and poked at the remaining beans on her plate. She wanted to steer the conversation more to her purposes. "Mr. Conti seemed pretty sad about his brother's death."

With that she began lining up the beans in a row across a puddle of reddish brown syrup.

Sonny swung one leg over the bench on his side of the picnic table. He pushed himself to a standing position by pressing against the table with the palms of his hands. As he did so, the muscles in his arms swelled beneath the cut-off sleeves of his sweatshirt. It occurred to Jocelyn that though Sonny might be a bit of a clown and even endearingly so when it came to playing the role of the outdoorsman, he probably wouldn't be such a pushover in other areas. Again, she felt a wave of uneasiness, as she had when she'd watched him struggle with the awning that morning.

"Did Clint tell you how Patrick died?" Sonny asked as he walked to the cooler he had set on the ground beside the trailer.

"He didn't seem to want to talk about it, and I didn't think I should ask." Jocelyn pushed the last bean into line. "Do you know how it happened?"

"Everybody up here knows about that." Sonny lifted the top of the cooler and pulled out another beer. The can shone wet with cold moisture in the lantern light. The pop and hiss of the top being removed was loud in the quiet evening. "Something that spectacular can't happen in a small town without people talking about it. Some of 'em are still talking about it...."

"I never heard anything."

Sonny had walked back to the table with the beer can in his hand. "It happened the middle of last August."

Jocelyn could tell he was watching her, though she continued staring at the row of elliptical brown beans in their puddle on her plate. Philip was killed the third week in August of last year. She remembered that she didn't believe in coincidences. She told herself that she did not believe in outlandish connections between disparate events, either. Her mother had been a great one for making wild assumptions about how everything was hooked up with everything else. According to her, it was all part of some cosmic design. According to Jocelyn, it was all baloney, but maybe in this case it wasn't.

"Patrick hit a tree on his motorcycle," Sonny said. He was still standing on the other side of the table looking down at her. "The police report said it was an accident."

Philip had died in an accident, too. Jocelyn's mother always used to say that there are no accidents.

"That's a nervous habit, you know," Sonny said.

"What?" Jocelyn looked up at him, startled.

He gestured toward her plate with his beer can. "Playing with your food like that. My ma used to tell me it was a nervous habit."

Sonny straddled the bench and lowered himself into the brightest part of the light from the lantern. Jocelyn was lit by the same bright light, and she could feel his eyes on her again.

"Could you turn that lamp down a little?" she asked. "It's starting to hurt my eyes."

"Sure."

Sonny turned the knob on the lantern obligingly, and the bright glow gradually subsided till there was only a soft illumination surrounding them and the darkness of the evening beyond that.

"Would you like to hear the Patrick Conti story?" Sonny asked.

"Is there more to it than the motorcycle accident?" Jocelyn asked, trying to sound only minimally interested.

"There's a lot more to it than that. And it starts before he died, too." Sonny took a swig from his can of beer. "Patrick had been suspended from the force just two or three weeks before he died. Some funny money was found hidden at his house."

"Counterfeit money?"

"That's right," Sonny said after another swig. "He had a bag of those fake twenties they've been running into downstate for the last couple of years. They think that shipments were coming across the border from Canada somewhere up north of here. Patrick Conti may have been mixed up in that somehow."

"But they don't know for sure that he was mixed up in it, do they?"

Sonny nodded. "That's right. Patrick bought the farm before the investigation had a chance to get very far off the ground. The Feds were into it after that since counterfeiting's a federal crime. The investigation hasn't gone much of anyplace since then as far as I know. Without Patrick, there was no witness and the bag of bills was the only real evidence they had. There weren't any fingerprints on those, either, so the whole thing bogged down after a while."

"So Patrick wasn't proven guilty, but he was never exonerated, either?"

"You got it," Sonny said, slapping the table for emphasis.

"That must have been hard on his family," Jocelyn said. She was thinking about one member of Patrick's family in particular.

"There was lots of talk around here, and his folks took a lot of heat. Guilty till proven innocent. That's how the system really works. Still, the talk started to die down after Patrick died. Except with the people who say that's why he hit that tree in the first place."

"I don't understand."

Clint leaned closer over the table. Unfortunately, the light was too low for her to read what was in his face even at this shorter distance.

"There were a number of folks around here, and still are, who believe Patrick drove his bike into that tree on purpose because he couldn't face the disgrace that was going to come down on him when he was indicted," Sonny said. "His arraignment had been scheduled to happen the week after he crashed his bike."

"That's just gossip, isn't it?" she asked. "There's no proof that Patrick committed suicide, is there?"

"Some people think there is. But it's more what wasn't found than what was found that makes them think maybe Patrick's dying wasn't any accident."

"What do you mean by what they didn't find?" Jocelyn asked. "What didn't they find where?"

"At the accident scene. By the tree. From the road-side up to the tree, to be exact." Sonny lifted his beer can to his mouth, leaned back his head and took a deep, long drink. His Adam's apple worked in his throat as the beer went down.

"What didn't they find by the tree?"

Sonny grasped his beer can in one hand and crushed it. He aimed the crumpled can at the brown paper bag and lobbed it easily in. Then he leaned close again in the lantern light.

"What they didn't find," he said, "was skid marks."

Chapter Ten

No skid marks! Jocelyn had watched enough cop shows and television news to understand that there were always skid marks in an accident—unless the driver had fallen asleep at the wheel. Could you fall asleep at the wheel of a motorcycle, with all that noise and vibration underneath you? Brake failure would be another explanation. What kind of brakes did a motorcycle have? Could they stop working in an instant like that? Wouldn't the steering have to fail, as well, in order to account for driving directly into a tree, if it was an accident?

The police report concluded that Patrick Conti met an accidental death. The police would have explored other avenues. Or might they have covered up the truth to spare the feelings of the family? After all, even with a possible blot on his record, Patrick was a policeman himself, one of their own, and everybody knew how the police could close ranks to protect one of their own.

The sound of loud rock and roll only intensified Jocelyn's reaction to what Sonny had told her.

"What is that?" Jocelyn asked above the din.

"There's a dance up at the campground pavilion tonight," Sonny said. "Somebody told me they have these events here pretty often."

Jocelyn remembered Philip's taking her out to dinner to avoid something like this last year.

"Come on. Let's check it out," Sonny said, hopping up from his side of the picnic table.

"Oh, I don't think so," Jocelyn began to protest.

Sonny hurried around the table and took hold of her arm. "Anything would be better than sitting around here having morbid thoughts and crying in your beer."

He had a point there.

"But I'm not really dressed for a dance." Jocelyn looked down at her T-shirt and jeans and toes sticking out of DeDe's thongs.

"This ain't my most formal sweatshirt, either. What do you think people wear to a campground dance? Ball gowns and tuxes?"

Another point for his side.

"Come on," he said, tugging her arm. "Let's give it a look. What have you got to lose?"

Jocelyn had been about to say that she wasn't in the mood for dancing and loud music, but maybe the mood she was in was exactly what she had to lose. She could use a break from today's emotional overload if only for a song or two.

"Okay," she said. "Let's give it a look."

"Good for you."

Sonny pulled a small comb from his back pocket and dragged it through his closely cropped hair. That reminded Jocelyn she had a wide-toothed comb in her jacket. She forced the teeth through her unruly hair, made thicker and curlier by the humidity and tangled from the flurry of today's activity. Her hair had also been tossed and blown during a couple of high-speed drives when personal appearance could hardly have been further from her mind. As she tugged at the comb, she couldn't help groaning in pain.

"You don't have to bother with that," Sonny said. "You look gorgeous."

Jocelyn stopped combing. She hoped Sonny didn't mean anything too personal by that. As usual, it hadn't occurred to her to consider that this man might look on her visit to his campsite as something more than a neighborly gesture on her part. Still, there had been nothing in his tone to indicate anything other than the jovial spirit that seemed to dominate Sonny's personality most of the time. If Clint Conti had told her she was gorgeous, she could imagine those words being spoken in a very different manner. She could hear his deep voice as surely as if he had been talking into her ear right now, and feel its timbre reverberating along her spine.

"Are you coming or not?" Sonny had let go of her arm and started up the hill toward the pavilion. He called out to her over his shoulder.

Thinking about Clint had put her in a disgruntled mood again. She didn't really want to go to the pavilion with Sonny, or anywhere with anyone, for that matter. Still, she didn't want to be rude. The least she could do was check out this dance for a few minutes with him. Then she could make her excuses and leave. Meanwhile, she was pleased to hear the music moderate to a softer level. Someone had probably complained already. That meant Jocelyn might have a realistic chance of some rest later on. For now, she followed Sonny up the hill toward the strains of Mick Jagger and "Honky-Tonk Woman."

The music would be mostly vintage rock and roll and country-western. That's what the sign outside the pavilion informed them. A local disc jockey who called himself Rockin' Ronnie had set up his equipment at one end of the long open-sided shed. He had even suspended a rotating mirrored disco ball from the center beam of the pavilion roof. Multicolored dots of light swirled over the crowd on the makeshift dance floor. Children jumped in circles together, and several mothers stepped and turned with babies in their arms.

A few couples, mostly teens, were also dancing together. They bounced and gyrated to the pounding beat of Charlie Watts on drums. Onlookers clapped and laughed from rows of picnic tables surrounding the dance area. Everybody appeared to be having a great time, and dress was as casual as Sonny had predicted it would be—jeans, shorts, T-shirts, even halter tops and lots of sandals just like Jocelyn's, kicking up the gravel as the end of one song blended directly into another without skipping a beat. The dancers shifted just as seamlessly, bumping and stomping to Creedence Clearwater Revival and "Bad Moon Rising."

"There's Hildy," Sonny shouted over the music crowd. He was pointing to the second row of picnic tables.

Jocelyn recognized the woman she had picked up on the road outside the quarry. Sonny was already waving to her and heading in her direction. Jocelyn thought she saw a look of what might be exasperation cross Hildy Hammond's face. Then she saw Jocelyn and it was gone.

"Hello, there," Hildy said, as Jocelyn came up to the table. "How good to see you again. I've been meaning to stop over at your trailer. I wanted to thank you once more for the other day. You practically saved my life, you know."

"You two have met each other?" Sonny asked.

"Yes, we have," Hildy said. There might have been some irritation in her voice, but it was hard to tell for sure in the surrounding noise. "Sit down," she said to Jocelyn.

Had Hildy deliberately excluded Sonny from that invitation? Again, it was hard to tell. Jocelyn suspected that the day's events had left her a bit paranoid, reading mysterious and perplexing undertones into perfectly innocent situations. Invited or not, Sonny plopped himself down on the opposite side of the table and turned to watch the flurry of activity on the dance floor. He drummed his fingers on the table in time to the music. If by some chance Hildy had meant to make him feel less than welcome, she had not succeeded.

"Just what the doctor ordered," he said, turning back to grin at Jocelyn. "Right, neighbor?"

"Right, neighbor," she answered, returning his smile.

Jocelyn was glad she had let Sonny talk her into coming here. The general high spirits of the crowd couldn't help but be a little infectious, even after a day like the one she had just lived through. She watched the children with their tanned, apple-cheeked faces. They clapped their hands and cavorted while parents kept an eye on them from the sidelines. Families grouped together with friends at the picnic tables. The disc jockey was handing out flexible neon wands in fluorescent fuchsia, electric green, bright blue and yellow. The children, and even a few of the adults, fashioned them into necklaces, halos and bracelets or twirled them over their heads. Jocelyn couldn't remember when she had last been part of such a festive gathering. It had been a very long time.

"I'll get us something to drink," Sonny said, pushing himself up from the table with that same muscle-flexing movement Jocelyn had noticed earlier. A pretty young woman was watching him with considerable interest from the next table, but Sonny looked past her without appearing to pay much attention.

"Nothing for me," Hildy said. She had brought a thermos with her and was sipping what looked like iced tea from the cup.

"I'll have a diet cola," Jocelyn shouted.

She had planned to go straight back to her trailer after a brief look at what was going on up here. Now, she thought she might stay awhile. The lightheartedness of the crowd was having its effect on her. Suddenly, she wasn't as tired as she had begun to feel at Sonny's campsite, especially after a few sips of beer. The music, the swirling lights, the sound of laughter and the sight of smiling faces all around her had stimulated a reserve source of energy she didn't know she had until this moment. Jocelyn was thinking that if Sonny asked her to dance, she just might give it a whirl.

There was another reason for joining the festivities, as well. Jocelyn knew it was time to put some distance between herself and Clint. She needed to be with other people and do things that didn't involve him in any way. She thought about him all too often. Being here tonight, with Sonny and Hildy and the other campground folk, would keep her mind clear of him. At least, she hoped so.

Then she saw Clint himself.

He was standing apart from the activity, at the back of the pavilion and just beyond the swirling circle of light, but Jocelyn had no trouble recognizing him. He was silhouetted against the trees behind him, which had been softly lit by low-set ground lights. That silhouette was tall, broad and unmistakable. A number of women had turned to look at him, some less subtly than others. Jocelyn couldn't see his face clearly in the semishadows, but she had the impression he was staring straight at her.

Clint began walking toward her, and she experienced what she could only describe as a rush of panic. Her heart fluttered in her throat. She swallowed hard to keep from gasping aloud. Her face was suddenly hot, and she was grateful for the darkness, which would hide the rising blush she was feeling. She looked around for a way out. The narrow aisle between the picnic tables was blocked in both directions by knots of people talking and laughing among themselves. Their pleasure seemed oddly foreign and out of place to Jocelyn, who could hardly have felt less jovial at this moment.

Meanwhile, Clint was getting closer, bearing down on her like inevitable doom. Sonny was also walking toward the table from the opposite direction, carrying a beer can in one hand and a soda can in the other. There was her way out. She would ask Sonny to dance. That would at least get her out of range of Clint's unrelenting approach. He was only a few yards away now and steadily closing that gap. She was about to stand up and shout her request at Sonny when the pretty young woman from the next table beat Jocelyn to the punch. The young woman stepped up to Sonny, took the two cans out of his hands and set them on the table, then linked her arm through his. Sonny raised his eyebrows toward Jocelyn and shrugged in an expression of surrender as he was led off to the dance floor.

Captured without a shot being fired, Jocelyn thought, envying the woman's aggressiveness with men, which she had never been able to master herself.

Clint was closer than ever. There would be no chance of escape now without a very conspicuous retreat. He was at her side and leaning down toward her. She debated whether making a run for it and worrying about the curious stares later might not be the best course of action. She heard him ask her to dance, but she didn't answer. Panic swept over her once more. Her legs had gone suddenly weak, and the invigoration she had caught from the crowd a few minutes ago was draining away.

She could hardly believe she was reacting so drastically. Maybe this was merely a delayed response to the many unsettling events of the day. Whatever the cause, she didn't answer him because she couldn't. Her mind wouldn't form the words for her mouth to speak. Then Hildy answered for her.

"Go ahead and dance," Hildy said. "Why would you want to sit on the sidelines with me? I'm only here to watch and listen anyway. Go have some fun."

Before Jocelyn could respond to that, Clint had taken her arm and was guiding her upward from the bench with an insistent pressure she felt powerless to resist. Hildy smiled up at Jocelyn. People at the nearby tables clapped and laughed and bounced their heads to the rhythm of the music. This was no place to make a scene. Besides, she'd had more than enough drama today. The easiest course of action in this awkward situation was to agree to dance with Clint. She told herself that the quickening of her pulse was caused by the tension of that awkwardness, nothing else.

They were almost at the edge of the dance floor when the music changed. Natalie Cole began to sing in long, languid tones about needing someone to watch over her. Jocelyn was thinking that was what she could use right now herself. She looked around for some alternative to the unnerving prospect of a slow dance with Clint. She spotted Sonny a few couples away. His pretty partner had wrapped her arms around his neck and draped her body along the length of his. Sonny gazed into her eyes in rapt attention, his surrender obviously absolute.

As for Jocelyn, she had no choice but to capitulate, as well. She should have run for her life when she had the chance. Now, it was too late. Clint put his arm around her waist and swept her against him. The strength of his embrace was startling. She wasn't prepared for the impact of being in his arms again, and not as one friend comforting another this time.

He was holding her very close. His hand had slipped up under the back of her jacket and pressed against the thin cotton of her T-shirt. The heat of his palm radiated through her so intensely that she suspected she might carry its imprint like a brand seared into her flesh forever. Her breasts crushed against him, and she tried to ignore the quick, aching thrill that discomfort sent trembling through her.

Yet, there could be no ignoring what was happening to her. She could not remember ever in her life experiencing such an immediate and intense sexual response to being held by a man. Even in the early days with Philip, when their relationship was new and fresh and should have been exciting, she had never felt anything like this. Every nerve in her body, every sense in her being had leaped to life. Jocelyn could hear her breath coming in short, fast gasps against the front of his shirt. She knew her nipples were hard as pebbles, yearning for his touch. She was sure that he must feel them against his chest and hear her ragged breathing. He must be able to guess what she was feeling, too. Jocelyn didn't want that. She willed her body to resist, but the ache in her belly only grew more intense and began turning to fire. Whatever doubts she had entertained, whatever anger she had felt toward him were being singed to ashes by that flame.

She glanced around. Sonny Shannon was still dancing nearby, but he was no longer gazing into his partner's eyes. He was looking straight at Jocelyn with a curious and questioning expression on his face. What did he see as he stared at her? What could possibly be in her eyes at this moment? Confusion? Terror? Desire? She cringed at the possibilities the nakedness of her current emotions presented.

Suddenly, she wanted to escape Sonny's gaze almost as much as she wanted to escape the torment of her hunger for Clint. She turned her face to his chest and buried it there. At the same moment she took the lead in their swaying motion long enough to turn him a half circle so that his body blocked Sonny's view of her. That movement caused Clint's thighs and pelvis to rub across her body even more closely than before. He must have taken this as an encouragement of his embrace, because he slid his hand down her spine to the hollow of her lower back and pressed her tightly against him.

She felt as well as heard the groan deep within his chest and couldn't keep herself from shuddering in response. Her face was hot and damp. She could feel the wisps of curl clinging to her cheeks and forehead. She was warm everywhere else, as well, as if she might melt into him at any moment and disappear there. What a seductive possibility that was—until a loud laugh close by brought her at least partway back to her senses and reminded her of where she was. They were on a public dance floor in the company of families with children.

Jocelyn lifted her face from Clint's chest and looked quickly around them. There were other couples dancing close. Nobody appeared to be paying any special attention to Clint and Jocelyn, though she couldn't understand why not. They had been locked in a definitely carnal embrace for several minutes now. She was surprised that everybody in the place wasn't staring at them with either shock or prurient interest. Yet, no one, with the possible exception of Sonny Shannon, had taken any particular notice at all.

Nonetheless, Jocelyn couldn't let this go on. She pushed herself out of Clint's arms and spoke as calmly as she could manage over the turmoil still raging inside her.

"I don't really feel like dancing right now," she said.

Clint retained his grip on her arm too tightly for her to pull it away without a fight. "Then let's walk," he said.

His voice was pitched even deeper than usual, as if he might be keeping it unnaturally low in order to keep in control of himself. Jocelyn sensed that his inner turmoil rivaled her own.

Clint propelled her through the dancers on the floor toward the rear of the pavilion, where he had been standing when Jocelyn first saw him earlier. She was grateful for that since it was the most direct route out of the lighted area. She didn't want even the flickers from the disco ball illuminating the confusion she was certain must show on her face and maybe elsewhere about her, as well. She wiped her free hand on her jeans and was dismayed to discover how supersensitized her touch had become, making her powerfully aware of every physical contact.

Clint led her through the crowd, out of the pavilion, past the circle of soft lighting and into the darkness of the surrounding trees. When she saw where they were headed, Jocelyn tried to pull away, but he would not let go of her. She had just decided that she would stop dead still and demand that he release her when he turned her to face him, locked his arms around her and covered her mouth with his.

They were both breathing hard into each other. Jocelyn struggled against his embrace. He held her tighter. She tried to wrench her mouth away from his. He grasped the back of her neck in his unyielding grip, and twist as she might, she could not escape his kiss. He was pressing his lips and body so hard and insistently against hers that he might have been attempting to imbed himself in her. She had never experienced being truly taken by a man. Now, she understood what that would be like.

Then suddenly Clint had relaxed his hold on her and turned almost gentle. His tongue explored hers. His hands cradled her face instead of entrapping it. He moved his lips from her mouth, trailing soft, moist but still insistent kisses over her chin and down her neck to the point where her pulse beat wildly in her throat. He touched his lips to that pulsating spot, and she sagged against him with a gasp.

Jocelyn was certain he was about to lift her off her feet and carry her into the woods, where they would act out her fantasy of earlier today, till their passion was mutually spent among the fallen leaves and pine needles on the forest floor. She told herself this must not happen. He was holding her so gently as he kissed her now that a great deal of physical strength was not needed to break away. Another kind of strength was required and all that she could muster of it. Her body cried out to join with his, to be engulfed by him in profound and delicious surrender. She ached and burned for that to come to pass, but something else burned inside her, as well. She had come to value herself too highly to give herself to a man who might not be worthy of her love and trust. She summoned all of her resistance and brought it to bear, not against Clint but against herself.

She pushed away from him and walked away as fast as she could. She heard him behind her, urging her to stop and talk. She also imagined that by now they must have attracted the attention of at least some of the people in the pavilion. For that reason only, she didn't break immediately into a run, but she was moving as fast as her thonged feet would carry her and still remain at a walk.

She had reached the front of the pavilion and was headed diagonally down the gradual slope in a direct line with her trailer. She was halfway to the road that bordered her campsite when Clint caught her by the arm and she had to halt, though she kept pulling in the direction she was headed, even managing to pull him along with her for a few steps.

"We have to talk about this," he said. "About what's happening between us."

"There's nothing happening between us," she said, more loudly than she had meant to, since they were moving beyond the loudest range of the music and into the vicinity of the campsites.

"You know that isn't true," Clint insisted. He was still holding fast to her arm.

Jocelyn did not turn to look at him. "I know that I want it to be true," she said.

She looked with longing toward the sanctuary of her trailer. The lamps on her deck glowed soft and welcoming. She had left them on to light her way home, and that was where she wanted to be right now.

But something was wrong. For a moment, she couldn't figure out exactly what it was. The chaos of this turbulent encounter with Clint had her confused, to say the least. Yet, she was certain that something wasn't right about her trailer. She stared at it, trying to collect her thoughts. Clint must have sensed this change of focus in her because he relaxed his grip on her arm and followed her gaze toward her campsite.

"What is it?" he asked. "What are you looking at?"

"The lights," she said. "I left the deck lights on, but that was all. Now there's a light on inside."

They were facing the front of her trailer at an angle. The French doors and the window over the dinette area were clearly visible. There was definitely a light shining through them from inside the trailer.

"Are you sure you didn't leave that light on, too?" Clint was asking, but Jocelyn had already broken free of his grasp and was running down the slope and across the road.

WHAT JOCELYN noticed first were the wildflowers. They stood out for her, for some reason, amid the

other, more significant chaos. There were storage
compartments beneath the seats in the dinette area of
her trailer. In order to get to those compartments, the
seat cushions had to be removed. That was supposed
to be done with care so as not to disturb the table and
whatever might be resting on it. Unfortunately, Jocelyn's visitor hadn't been at all concerned with taking
care. He had yanked up the seat cushions so hard that
the tabletop was dislodged from its legs and thrown up
against the window. The small vase full of wildflowers
had been thrown as well, scattering its contents over an
askew dinette cushion and onto the carpeted floor of
the living room area.

Jocelyn bent down slowly, in a daze, to pick up the
purple, yellow and pink blossoms. She straightened
their fractured stems in her hand, as if by doing so she
might undo the wreckage someone had made of the
summer home she loved so well. This had been her
sanctuary. This had been the corner of her world that
was completely her own. She had paid for it. She had
decorated it. She had shared it with others only rarely
and always at her own choosing—until this evening,
sometime within the past couple of hours. During that
time, someone had invaded her sanctuary. They had
tossed her belongings here and there, pulled the contents from drawers and cupboards, and created general disorder.

The Delaneys called the sheriff's office for her.
When the deputy arrived, the whirling red light on top
of his patrol car must have been brighter and more
compelling than the flicker from the disco ball because a crowd had streamed down the hill from the
pavilion with Sonny Shannon and Hildy Hammond
among them. Clint had been with Jocelyn from the

moment she pushed through the open sliding door and found this mess. He had run after her when she first took off toward the trailer. He caught up with her when she was about to rush onto the deck. Clint wouldn't let her do that. He was the one to slip cautiously inside and make certain the intruder was gone before Jocelyn came in.

So, she wasn't alone as she faced the havoc. However, she felt alone, and she felt afraid. She knew this was not a random attack of thieves or vandals. Though the deputy said there had been other break-ins around the area during the past several weeks, including two at this campground, Jocelyn was sure that these incidents had nothing to do with what had happened here tonight. Nothing had been stolen. Beyond the disarray created by a thorough and hasty search, there was no attempt to deface her property, no deliberately smashed belongings or graffiti scrawls. Whoever was here earlier had been looking for something. Even the deputy agreed with that.

The deputy was much more skeptical about Jocelyn's suggestion that this break-in was connected somehow with all of the strange and unsettling things that had been going on in her life these past few days. He took down everything she told him. He claimed that the sheriff's department would investigate further. When she insisted, with a hint of hysteria in her plea, that they look into Philip's activities while using the name Reggie Williams, the deputy finally said they would. Still, Jocelyn could tell that he thought the situation with Philip was nothing more than a case of a private domestic conflict involving some marital infidelity, not the kind of thing the police generally involve themselves with. The deputy went along with her request mostly to keep her calm, but he did give her his word that he would follow up on what she had told him.

Even so, Jocelyn couldn't help being reminded, in a very frightening way, of a dream she used to have repeatedly when she was growing up, living with her flaky mother. In that dream, Jocelyn would know that something terrible had happened. She hadn't seen what it was. She only knew that something hideous had occurred and she needed help desperately. She would run from door to door, knocking and screaming and begging for somebody to come to her aid, but no one would believe there was any danger. No matter how emotional her entreaties, no matter what lengths she went to convince them, no one but herself could or would understand the peril she was in. Eventually Jocelyn would wake up and find herself in her bed, among the objects she recognized as belonging to her bedroom. Yet, she would feel as if she were in some foreign place, terrified and alone.

Jocelyn felt a lot like that now. Later, it would occur to her that Clint was the one person who might have been able to alleviate some of that fear and isolation. Instead, he had kept himself aloof from most of what was going on, especially after the sheriff's deputy arrived. She was periodically aware of Clint at the periphery of things, watching but not involving himself further than that. Suddenly, she had the strong impression of his being like one of those doors in her dream, which she might knock upon till her knuckles were bloody but there would be no response from inside. In this instance at least, for some reason, Clint would be like all the rest. He would leave her terrified and alone.

Chapter Eleven

"Do you have somewhere else to stay tonight?" the sheriff's deputy was asking Jocelyn.

She hadn't thought about that yet. The police had completed their investigation, which was really more a look around than an intensive inquiry. Jocelyn had accompanied the deputy out onto the deck as he prepared to leave. That was when she noticed the basket of impatiens. It had been hanging over the deck. Now it was on the ground with dirt and blossoms spilled around it. Someone had actually dug into the densely packed, moist potting soil and scooped most of it out. Jocelyn was reminded of old black-and-white World War II vintage espionage movies where the enemy spies, or sometimes even the good guys, hid the microfilm in some otherwise mundane spot—like a hanging planter of impatiens.

The image of Ray Milland grubbing through her potted plants almost set Jocelyn off into a gale of giggles. She suspected that hysteria might be behind this impulse to giggle. In the next instant, the urge to laugh had passed and she was just as afraid that she might cry instead. She felt her eyes awash with tears, and sobs had already filled her throat.

"She can stay with me." Hildy Hammond was at the foot of the steps to Jocelyn's deck. "I have plenty of room."

This was the second time Hildy had offered to help this evening. Earlier, when Jocelyn was inside the trailer surveying the damage, Hildy had appeared at the door asking what she could do. The deputy had stopped her from coming inside, where she might disturb the evidence he was supposedly investigating. Hildy left as he directed, but Jocelyn now recalled the reluctance with which Hildy had done so. There had been a look of true concern in her eyes that told Jocelyn here was somebody who might take her plight seriously. Here was a door she might knock upon and be believed.

The deputy walked down the steps from the deck just as Hildy moved tentatively up to them. "You might want to take her up on that offer," he said, nodding at Hildy while also giving her a once-over glance with a wry expression on his face.

Hildy was something of a sight. She had pulled on a faded Mexican serape over her work shirt and drawstring pants. Her feet were clad in an old, stretched-out pair of men's argyle socks and shoved into huaraches. Jocelyn could only imagine what the inside of Hildy's trailer might look like. Maybe the Delaneys would be a better prospect for a bed for the night, at least until Jocelyn's locks had been replaced in the morning.

She was searching for a way to suggest that without being rude to Hildy, when Clint stepped forward from the dwindling group of onlookers. Something in his face told Jocelyn that he might be about to suggest that he could put her up for the night himself.

"Thank you, Hildy," Jocelyn said as hastily as she could get the words out. "If you're sure I won't be inconveniencing you, I'd be grateful for the help, just for tonight."

"You won't be inconveniencing me at all, dear," Hildy said, patting Jocelyn's arm. "We'll be cozy as two bugs in a rug."

Jocelyn wasn't at all sure that cozying up with Hildy was desirable. Nonetheless, she was offering a readily available port in a storm, and Jocelyn was glad for the opportunity to sail into it. Out of the corner of her eye, she saw Clint halt his approach. He thrust his hands into his jeans pockets and watched the scene on the deck in silence for a moment longer, then turned and walked off toward the road. Her ploy with Hildy had worked. A recollection of what had happened behind the pavilion when she was in Clint's arms flashed through her and she shivered in unbidden response.

"You're going to catch a chill out here," Hildy said, bustling up the last step to the deck. She pulled her serape over her head, sending her hair into even wilder disorder than usual. "Put this on."

She draped the serape, shawl-style, over Jocelyn's shoulders. She might have resisted such maternal attention, but she was preoccupied with Clint's broad back moving up the slope and receding into the darkness. Jocelyn shivered again at the realization of just how conflicted her feelings were where he was concerned.

"You *are* catching a chill," Hildy said. Her arm was around Jocelyn's shoulders urging her toward the steps. "My place is nice and warm and I have everything you need there, even a fresh toothbrush. You just come along with me right now."

Jocelyn was only half listening to Hildy's chatter. Then she said something that was a real attention getter, even in Jocelyn's benumbed state. Hildy leaned closer and spoke in hushed tones, apparently to prevent the deputy from hearing.

"I also have something to tell you that may shed some light on what happened here tonight," she said.

Jocelyn opened her mouth to question further, but Hildy put a finger to her lips to signal silence. The deputy was no longer paying much attention, so he didn't notice. The Delaneys had volunteered to put a temporary barricade across the sliding doors to Jocelyn's trailer. They were busy attending to that. The last of the curious onlookers were straggling away as the deputy closed his memo pad and slid his pen back into his shirt pocket. That obviously wrapped up any official business on his part.

Jocelyn cast a glance back into the remains of her living room. There really wasn't anything left for her to do here tonight. The get-right-to-it part of her would have liked to set about sorting out the mess immediately. Fortunately, her common sense told her she wasn't up to that just yet, either physically or psychologically. Better to put a good night's sleep between now and the unpleasant task. Just as it was a good idea to put some distance between herself and Clint Conti until she'd had a chance to sort out some things in that department, as well.

"Let's go," she said to Hildy and continued down the steps ahead of the older woman.

Jocelyn wasn't pleased at the way Clint popped into her thoughts so readily and so often. Maybe getting a move on would shake him out of her consciousness for a while. With that purpose in mind, she hurried toward the road with Hildy bustling along at her side. Still, Jocelyn had her doubts that thoughts of Clint would be easy to leave behind, no matter how fast she might run. She clutched the makeshift shawl more tightly about her shoulders to ward off yet another shiver.

HILDY'S TRAILER was several sites down the road. She wasn't surprised to find that Hildy hadn't made any attempt to develop or beautify her site—no decks or flowers or outdoor furniture. The lawn was free of debris and recently mowed but barren. Of course, Hildy was only renting the site on a temporary basis. She had mentioned that the other morning in the car. She was also here for work rather than vacation and probably didn't have time for much else.

The inside of her trailer was proof of that. The dinette area had been set up as a laboratory table, complete with microscope and tagged specimens. Labels on the cupboard doors organized the shelves according to what artifacts had been categorized there. Hildy had even made use of the dish strainer by filing her journals in the plate slots. There were books just about everywhere, stacked on the refrigerator and across one dinette seat.

"Believe it or not, I know right where everything is," Hildy said as Jocelyn gazed around at the office and laboratory Hildy had so ingeniously fashioned in such a limited space. "And right now I'm most pleased that I know where the coffeepot is."

Hildy took a tin of coffee from the small refrigerator and a plastic gallon bottle of water from under the dinette table and began spooning coffee into the aluminum percolator on the stove. She kept her foodstuffs in the lower cupboard, and some rummaging in there produced three separate bags containing three different kinds of cookies. Hildy pulled out cups and saucers and a plate for the cookies, all of beige-white china with scalloped edges and a border of pink rosebuds.

"Relics from the genteel world," Hildy said as she set down the pretty cups and saucers on a low table in front of the couch.

Jocelyn was surprised to find no books or research equipment in the alcove that served as a living room. She was also surprised and pleased to find that she and Hildy shared a love of bringing some of the finer things of life to the wilderness.

"I have blue dishes in my trailer," she said, "but they're stoneware, not china."

"As long as they aren't paper. I don't care to have my plate absorb as much of my meal as I do."

Jocelyn smiled. The pot was perking merrily already, and the smell of good coffee had begun to bring her back to life. Suddenly ravenous, she picked up a chocolate chip cookie from the plate and restrained herself from devouring it in two bites.

"I keep this area free of my clutter," Hildy said, setting the matching china sugar bowl and creamer on the table next to the cookie plate. "Otherwise, I would feel more like a dog in a junkyard than a person. A human being needs a corner set aside just for being human in, I always say."

Jocelyn nodded. Her trailer used to be that corner where her life was concerned. She hoped that before long she would be able to think of it that way again.

"This sofa pulls out into a bed," Hildy said. "I sleep out here some nights. I'm going to do that tonight and have you take the bedroom."

Jocelyn started to protest, but Hildy waved for silence. "That's the way I want it," she said. "I get up in the middle of the night on occasion to work. That's the way it is with lots of people my age. We don't need anywhere near as much sleep as we used to. So, it's better for you to bunk in there." She pointed to a door at one end of the trailer. "That way I won't disturb you when I start rattling around in here during the wee hours."

"Thank you," Jocelyn said. She really did feel better about sleeping in a room with a door on it.

"Let me get you something to put on in the meantime."

The coffeepot was perking loudly now. Hildy adjusted the stove flame a bit lower as she bustled past toward the bedroom end of the trailer. A few minutes later she came hurrying back with her arms full.

"This is for sleeping." She held up a lovely, old-fashioned white cotton nightgown with smocked bodice and ruffles at the neck opening and cuffs. The extra material required for Hildy's girth would make the gown hang long enough on much thinner Jocelyn to compensate for the inches she was taller than Hildy.

"Here's something for your shoulders in case you sit up in bed at night and read like I do." She handed Jocelyn a blue knitted shawl to replace the folded serape she still had around her shoulders. "I noticed from my glance into your trailer that you like blue."

"It's my favorite color," Jocelyn said. She was touched by Hildy's attentive kindness.

"Something to prevent cold feet." Hildy held out a pair of men's argyle socks much like her own. "Sorry they aren't too feminine, but I generally opt for serviceability where footwear is concerned."

Jocelyn smiled. "They're fine."

"And this is for right now." Hildy gave Jocelyn an oversized crew-neck sweater, also blue. "Why don't you pull that on over your T-shirt. I think you might need it, judging by the way you were shivering back on that deck of yours."

Jocelyn took the sweater. It was soft from many wearings and washings. She would have liked to talk with somebody, especially another woman, about the real reason for her shivering, but she wasn't ready for that yet. Instead, she took Hildy's advice and, after discarding the serape, pulled on the blue sweater, which smelled like clean laundry and sunshine.

Hildy had put on an oven mitt and taken the pot from the stove. She carried the pot to the table by the couch and poured steaming strong coffee into the two china cups. She set the pot on a trivet and sat down on the sofa with Jocelyn.

"Do you feel up to talking?" Hildy asked. "Or would you rather get straight to sleep?"

"Oddly enough, I'm not sleepy. I probably should be, but I'm not."

"That happens sometimes when a body's been through a tense time. The nerve endings snap to attention and tend to stay that way for a while. You just have to give yourself a chance to wind down. Then you might very well sleep the clock around."

"You could be right about that." The thought sounded tempting to Jocelyn, but she knew that if she went to bed now she would lie there staring at the ceiling till dawn. "How about you? Are you tired?"

"Not a bit." She was spooning so much sugar into her cup that Jocelyn could understand why Hildy was so energized, between the glucose and the caffeine. "I feel like a chat if you do."

"I was hoping you would tell me what you were referring to back at my trailer, when you said you might know something about the break-in."

"I told you a bit about it the other day, when you gave me a ride back here from the quarry."

Jocelyn put her cup down in its saucer. "I don't understand. Are you saying that you knew about this break-in before it happened?"

"Not exactly," Hildy said slowly. "I just knew that *things* were going to happen but not precisely what they would be."

"I still don't understand."

Jocelyn had begun to grow skeptical. She tried to remember what Hildy had said that morning in the car. There had been something about her research into local Indian tribes. She preferred that they be called native Americans. Jocelyn remembered that. There had been something else, too, but she couldn't quite put her finger on it. After the overload her psyche had suffered lately, she wouldn't have been surprised if her memory stopped functioning altogether.

"I tried to tell you about an experience I had at the quarry," Hildy said. "I could tell you didn't believe it, and I can't blame you for that. I didn't really believe it myself. But I've gone back there since, and now I'm convinced I wasn't imagining what happened. There is some kind of... being in that quarry, and for some reason I sense that it has something to do with the break-in at your trailer tonight.''

Jocelyn sighed. Now she remembered the conversation with Hildy in the car. She had been babbling about some kind of presence. Bits and pieces of what she had said were coming back to Jocelyn. According to Hildy, she had been engulfed by whatever it was. That's how she had described it. She was right about Jocelyn's not putting much stock in that story then, and she felt the same way now. She was also disappointed. She had come over here thinking she might gain some insight or pick up a clue, no matter how small, into the bizarre events of not only this evening but of the past few days, as well. Instead, she was being subjected to half-baked New Age hogwash about presences or ghosts or whatever.

She felt a little guilty for having such uncharitable thoughts about Hildy while accepting her very gracious hospitality. Jocelyn just couldn't help getting frustrated. She had allowed herself the wild hope that Hildy, with her microscopes and scientist's mind, might provide a key to all the recent craziness in her life.

It occurred to Jocelyn that maybe she was crazy herself, like a fanatical conspiracy theorist who sees patterns and plots everywhere. She was no better than Hildy with her theories about being communicated with by supernatural beings. What Jocelyn had been thinking was only a little less far out of the realm of probability.

"Come with me," Hildy was saying. "I know it's a lot to ask, but if you would just come to the quarry with me you might be able to help me figure out what is going on there, or maybe what isn't."

"All right," Jocelyn said. "I'll go there with you."
She stood up and looked down at Hildy. "Let's go."

"Right now?" Hildy asked, sounding as if she couldn't believe what she was hearing. "At night?"

"We'll take flashlights. If a presence is there as you say, or a spirit, wouldn't night be the best time to look for him?"

Hildy stood up slowly from the couch. "I didn't expect that you would be the one talking me into this."

"I wouldn't have expected it myself."

Hildy still hung back, her stance uncertain and slightly off-balance between the sofa and the table with its china coffee service. "Then why are you doing this?"

Jocelyn thought for a moment before answering. "Let's just say I'm trying to find my way out of a nightmare."

HILDY HAD BROUGHT a high-powered electric lantern, the kind with a handle on top. Jocelyn carried a more ordinary flashlight that she found in the glove compartment of the Lincoln.

It had begun to rain. Jocelyn pulled what bad weather gear she had from the car trunk—a hooded rain jacket for herself and a waterproof poncho for Hildy. Her own rain boots were still in the back seat, but she didn't dare open up her blister again by putting them on. The rain was warm, anyway. Her feet wouldn't be cold even in DeDe's thong sandals.

They had turned onto the access road into the quarry. It wasn't until Jocelyn killed the engine and turned off the lights that she started to wonder what she was doing here. Back at Hildy's trailer, this trip had seemed like a good way to burn off excess adrenaline.

There had also been the excitement of an anticipated adventure, as if they were adolescents sneaking
out at night to explore after everybody else was asleep.
Now that she was here, that excitement had been replaced by the realization that she was in a dark, unfa-
miliar place in the rain with only an eccentric old
woman for a companion.

Jocelyn eased the car door shut to avoid making any
loud noises in the surrounding silence. Hildy apparently had no such qualms and gave her door a hard
slam that made Jocelyn jump. She pulled her hood
forward to keep her head dry, then pushed the hood
partway back again so that the sides wouldn't obstruct
her vision. There wasn't much to see, just the shadowy
shapes of tree trunks she could barely make out in the
overcast darkness. She snapped on her flashlight and
was dismayed at how little illumination it provided.
Fortunately, Hildy's lantern shed a strong, wide beam.
She had taken the lead as they began their trek to the
quarry. Jocelyn stumbled over a rock and stubbed her
toe before she realized that she had to train her own
light on the ground directly in front of her and keep it
there.

Scrub grass had grown up among the jagged clusters of broken rock and gravel that covered the quarry
floor. Jocelyn wondered what had been quarried here.
Gravel was often used for blacktopping county roads.
The ones around here would require patches and re-
surfacing after the ravages of each harsh north country winter. Whatever its former use, this particular
quarry had been abandoned some time ago and left for
nature to reclaim.

Jocelyn swept her light along the walls that bordered two sides of the quarry's stone floor. Saplings

were growing out of clefts in the striated rock. The third side of the quarry was only part stone. The earthen section of that wall must have been the site of Hildy's digging. There were visible signs of recent excavation near the center of the embankment. Hildy was headed in that direction, pursuing a winding path over the quarry floor. She must be avoiding fissures or other obstacles, Jocelyn thought.

Jocelyn couldn't see clearly enough to tell exactly what Hildy might be doing. The summer shower had intensified to a downpour. Rivulets streamed off Jocelyn's hood and into the neck opening of her jacket. She pulled the hood forward once more to avoid getting drenched. That obscured her view even further. She looked toward Hildy's light bobbing at the other side of the quarry. Jocelyn was now more doubtful than ever that she should have come on this jaunt in the first place. What she heard next was enough to convince her that she would have been wiser to stay home.

The sound came from somewhere ahead and above the level of the quarry floor, as if it might be drifting down from the trees—or maybe from the heavens. More likely, the sound had originated from the rim of the quarry, along the top of the wall where Jocelyn had noticed evidence of an excavation. Hildy had gone off in that direction, but she wasn't in the right position to be the source of the sound. What would Hildy be doing playing music, anyway?

Jocelyn was definitely hearing music. She could make out only isolated notes at first. The rain was driving down hard now, drumming against her hood and jacket. She pulled the hood out from her ear and listened intently. What she heard made her stop in her tracks and stand very still. Could she trust her ears when what they told her was so bizarre?

The isolated musical notes had organized themselves into a recognizable tune. Jocelyn sucked in her breath in disbelief. This could not be happening. Someone was playing a flute, and the song they were playing was "Greensleeves." Jocelyn listened a moment to make certain this incredible realization was true.

Two things made this occurrence especially bewildering for Jocelyn. First of all, she knew enough about the flute and its system of valves and openings to know that it would be nearly impossible to play one in this very heavy rainstorm, much less to do so this clearly and infallibly. Since it takes both hands to play a flute, the flautist couldn't possibly be holding an umbrella to shield the instrument from the rain. There could be someone accompanying the flute player, and that second person might be holding the umbrella. But why would anybody do such a thing in this deluge?

The second source of Jocelyn's bewilderment was even more perplexing. It had to do with her late husband, Philip. He had not been much of a devotee of culture. Art and theater generally left him cold. He did, however, have a limited appreciation of music. That appreciation had begun in adolescence when his mother had badgered him into taking music lessons. He didn't progress very far in those studies. He never even got to the point where he was accomplished enough to try out for the school orchestra. Nonetheless, he had kept his instrument, even after he married Jocelyn. Once in a while he would take it out and play the one song he had been able to master back in junior high school. Jocelyn had heard him do that a number of times, usually when he was upset about something and attempting to calm himself.

The instrument Philip kept in a scarred leather case on his closet shelf was a flute. The one song he could play on it was "Greensleeves."

Chapter Twelve

Jocelyn didn't believe in ghosts. She was not her mother's daughter in that respect. Jocelyn didn't have metaphysical experiences herself, and she didn't think that other people really had them, either. Testimony to the contrary she would chalk up to emotionalism, susceptibility to suggestion or just plain deceit. Maybe she had fallen under the influence of one or both of the first two elements. There could be no other explanation for what was happening, at least none she could accept.

"Jocelyn," a voice called through the rain.

Too high-pitched to be Philip, Jocelyn thought, then couldn't believe her own mind. Philip was dead and gone. What was wrong with her?

Still, the voice didn't sound like Hildy's even when it called out again. Jocelyn strained to see through the rain and dark. She was relieved to find the lamp, faint at first, then stronger, bobbing toward her across the quarry.

"Do you hear the music?" the call came once more.

It was Hildy, after all. Her voice must have been distorted by the rain or perhaps by the anxiety Jocelyn could already detect there.

"Yes, I hear it," Jocelyn called back.

She stopped to listen. Actually, the music had stopped, though the echo of it lingered in the air. Jocelyn felt rather than heard that resonance, as if the vibrations of flute sound had filled the quarry and been trapped there by the downpour. She might have told herself she had imagined the whole thing, except that Hildy had heard it, too. Jocelyn might accept the possibility of an auditory hallucination experienced by one person, but not two, especially not two people the distance of a deep quarry apart.

Hildy was visible now, running a few steps, then walking in between before she could run again. She was stooped forward and heaving, as if she was struggling to catch her breath from exertion and maybe fear. She was also babbling something, but Jocelyn couldn't make out what it was.

"Speak more slowly, Hildy," she said. "I can't understand you."

Hildy came stumbling up to Jocelyn and took hold of her arm. Hildy leaned there for support while she gulped in air in furtive gasps. She was nearly doubled over. Jocelyn tried to take the lantern because Hildy looked as if she was about to drop it, but she wouldn't let go. She clung to the lantern with one hand and to Jocelyn's arm with the other.

Jocelyn dropped her own flashlight and tried to grasp Hildy under the arms to support her.

"No," Hildy cried out between gasps and jerked free from Jocelyn. "Don't hold on to me. I have to get out of here."

She straightened up some and pulled the poncho around her. She obviously wasn't yet sufficiently recovered from her dash across the quarry to start moving again, but she was just as obviously on her mark to take off the instant she was able.

"Did something happen to you in there?" Jocelyn asked. "Something besides the music?"

Hildy snapped her head up to glare at Jocelyn. "It *was* the music," Hildy said. Her poncho hood had slipped off when she made that sudden movement. Rain pelted her face, but she didn't seem to notice. "It's too strong this time. We can't stay here."

The rain had already drenched her hair and plastered it in saturated clumps against her scalp. Water ran off each clump, down her neck and over her ears. Jocelyn reached out to empty the puddle of rain water from Hildy's hood and pull it back over her head.

"Don't be helping me." She batted Jocelyn's hand away. "Help yourself. You're the one who needs it."

"What are you talking about?"

Hildy tightened her grip on Jocelyn's arm and started pulling hard. "Come with me now. We have to get out of here. We'll talk later."

Hildy was pulling so insistently that she dragged Jocelyn along for a few steps till she deliberately planted herself, digging her heels into the softer ground near the edge of the quarry floor. "Stop, Hildy," she said. "Tell me what we are running away from. Did you see somebody back there in the quarry?"

"No*body*," Hildy cried out with unmistakable emphasis. "But something is there, all right, and it is after *you*."

"That's ridiculous."

Jocelyn ignored the sudden catch in her throat. She reminded herself that she didn't believe in the disembodied. She was the rational one. She was not her mother. She was not Hildy Hammond, either.

"Have it your way, then," Hildy said. "I'm getting out of here."

Before Jocelyn could respond, Hildy had started off again. Her poncho billowed out behind her in the wind gusts that had now begun to accompany the rain. She took the lantern with her, leaving Jocelyn in darkness.

"Hildy, wait," Jocelyn called out after the stumbling, departing figure. "Wait till I find my flashlight."

Hildy didn't appear to have heard. She scrambled off into the gloom. The rain was being whipped in heavy sheets by the wind. In what seemed like mere seconds, Hildy was lost from view and her lantern along with her. Jocelyn peered into the rainswept night but could make out nothing through the gusting torrent.

She was standing in the water and mud that was collecting atop the hard ground. She was still on the quarry floor but near the point where stone and gravel gave way to grassy earth. The legs of Jocelyn's jeans were being soaked by the blowing rain, clear up to midthigh where her rain jacket ended.

Hildy was right. It was time to get out of here. Jocelyn walked back a few steps into the quarry, near as she could guess to where she had dropped her flashlight. She felt around with one thonged foot, but that did no good. She bent forward to study the ground, but she couldn't make out anything very clearly. Finally she reached out with both hands and searched with her fingertips in one last-ditch effort. She might just have to stumble out of here in the blackness and take her chances on ending up somewhere close to the place where she had parked her car.

She touched metal and her heart leaped with relief. She grasped the cylinder greedily.

"Damn," she cursed into the wind. It was only a discarded soda can. She tossed it away in exasperation.

As she stooped forward, rain poured off the front edge of her rain hood and splattered on the ground at her feet. Her jacket had pulled up in the back. Now her jeans were soaking wet up over her buttocks and almost to her waist. She was suddenly aware of being very uncomfortable and growing more so by the minute. To hell with the flashlight. She was going to find her way out of here if she had to do it on her hands and knees.

Jocelyn straightened up from her crouch, directly into a gust of rain with a strong push of wind behind it. The gust hit her full in the face. She was being drenched as completely and startlingly wet as if someone had turned on a faucet and stuck her head underneath it. She hesitated while another kind of drenching overtook her, just as complete and even more startling.

Hildy's description from that first morning in the truck popped into Jocelyn's head. *Engulfed!* She was being engulfed!

Hildy had also said it wasn't an unpleasant experience, but that wasn't Jocelyn's impression. To her, this was very unpleasant, indeed, especially since she had no idea what could be happening. And the feeling was frighteningly familiar. Philip.

Philip was generally a self-possessed person. He almost never got rattled or anxious. He made it a practice to be certain he was in total control of whatever was happening. Therefore, anxiety wasn't necessary. Only on the extremely rare occasion when he couldn't help but be dependent on somebody else would Philip's placid facade show any sign of disturbance.

Jocelyn remembered those few times when he'd had to depend on her for something or other. She also remembered how he had behaved then and how it had felt to be with him. In those situations, he had given off a palpable sense of crisis, like an inescapable message beam emanating from him in powerful waves and crying out, "Do this now. Do it right. Do it, anyway." And he'd spoken in a tone so compelling that it would strike fear in her heart.

She felt that fear grip her now. She clutched the front of her jacket and pulled it close around her as she glanced quickly to the right and left. She knew she would see nothing in either direction. Some thin thread of rational thought remained at her disposal. Beyond that narrow margin, all she knew was that what she used to feel emanating from Philip in crucial moments when he wasn't in total control was exactly what she felt now. A sense of urgency was engulfing her.

Jocelyn had frozen where she stood, like an outgrowth of the quarry floor as permanent and petrified as the layers of the prehistoric rock beneath her feet. She was rooted there, as if a force from deep within the molten center of the earth had blasted up through a million years of striations and shackled her feet to this bit of ground.

Then the possibility of salvation presented itself. It came in the form of a flash of knowledge so intense that it flooded away all doubt. Jocelyn had no idea where this pronouncement had come from. She only knew that it was true.

You must get off the quarry floor, it told her. *This presence only has power within these rocky walls.*

Jocelyn didn't stop to question the authenticity of that voice or to reject the plausibility of what was happening to her, as she would ordinarily have done. Instead, she bolted up to stand as straight and tall as possible. She would need every inch of her physical stature and every ounce of her emotional strength to do what had to be done.

She stretched her arms in front of her, palms open and pressed outward as if pushing against a great barrier or a prison wall. She took a deep breath and lunged forward. She willed all of her momentum into the palms of her hands and launched herself off the spot where she had been so implacably planted a moment before. She shoved against that barrier that only her mind's eye could see and carried the rest of herself along by the sheer determination of her effort.

There was resistance to her movement. Later on, she would tell herself it must have been the wind, but at the moment she did not attempt to define her adversary. Something or someone was attempting to prevent her from escaping a place where she no longer wanted to be. She pitted herself against the adversary each struggling step along hard, fissured rock and shale until she reached muddy ground.

Jocelyn didn't stop at that point. She stumbled a few yards farther before sinking to her knees in the resilient earth. The battle that had just transpired might have taken seconds or hours. She couldn't tell. She only knew she had triumphed over her opposition.

Sobs of relief and gratitude welled up inside her. She was about to let them burst forth into the fury of the storm when something grabbed her beneath the armpits and started hauling her to her feet. Panic jolted through her, but she swallowed it fast along with the sobs.

Her so-called flash of knowledge had spoken wrong, maybe even deliberately deceived her for some unfathomably cruel reason. The force that had surrounded her on the quarry floor did have power beyond that place. It was here trying to drag her back there at the very moment. She must not let that happen.

Jocelyn had heard north country people talk of being bone tired. Now she understood exactly what they had meant by that. She also understood she had to ignore that exhaustion and surge past it as if it were not weighting her arms and legs with tons of weariness. She must not think about that. She must not think about anything. She must only fight.

She had been dragged nearly upright when the fierceness of her resolve kicked in. She planted her feet beneath her and began to struggle. She twisted and flailed so furiously that she broke the grip beneath her arms long enough to swing around and face her attacker. She couldn't see very clearly through the rain and wind and her own rage. She only registered that whatever had grabbed her was visible and tangible, all right. It was also large and solid, set down between her and the quarry floor like a massive boulder or a tall tree trunk.

She might have turned and fled, back in the direction where she still sensed that safety lay, out at the roadside and off away from this accursed place. She would do that in a moment. But first she had to plant one blow of her own.

She would have kicked out with all her might, but she remembered that she was wearing only thongs on bare wet feet. She ducked fast and ran her fingers swiftly along the ground. In only inches she touched what she was searching for. She grasped it firmly and straightened back up, arcing her arm as she rose, projecting the force of her entire body behind that movement. Her fist and the rock inside it were at their apex and descending into a crashing blow when a grip as hard as cold steel caught her wrist.

"Jocelyn, stop! It's me!"

She geared herself for yet another battle, maybe even harder pitched than the last. She heard the voice and thought she knew it.

"Jocelyn, it's me! It's Clint!"

She hesitated just long enough for a slender needle of ordinary reality to pierce the intensity of what she had been experiencing since she entered this quarry what felt like a separate lifetime ago. Without knowing exactly why, she reached up with her free hand and touched the face above her. He flinched at first, as if expecting she might be about to scratch out his eyes. Instead, she moved her fingers tentatively up his cheek, over the strong bridge of his nose, then back along the ridge that shielded his deeply set eyes.

There was no mistaking whose face this was. She would have known it anywhere, even without seeing it. The sobs that filled her chest earlier hadn't dissipated, after all. They burst forth now as Jocelyn flung her arms around Clint's neck and buried her face in his rain-soaked jacket. She had willed every sinew in her body taut and ready to take on her enemy. Despite her earlier suspicions, she knew at this moment Clint was on her side. Her tension released like a bowstring suddenly broken. She sagged against Clint. He caught her in his arms, and she took refuge there. Only the fingers of her right hand refused to abandon their preparedness for combat. They remained clenched around the rock she had picked up, the only weapon of defense she had.

CLINT HAD INSISTED on taking them to his house because it was closer to the quarry than the campground was. He said that Jocelyn needed to get somewhere warm fast. She didn't argue. She hadn't said much of anything since he pried the stone from her hand and half-led, half-carried her out of the quarry to his truck. He wrapped her in a blanket from behind the seat while Hildy scrambled up next to her.

Jocelyn was vaguely aware of the two of them watching her all the way to Clint's house. He kept stealing glances at her, then driving even faster than before. The rain had let up a little, but he was still well over the speed he should be traveling on such slick roads. Jocelyn remembered when she had driven recklessly the first time she met Hildy and how nervous that had made her. Hildy wasn't complaining now.

When they reached their destination, Clint stopped the truck and hurried around to help the women out of the other side of the cab. He handed Hildy down first.

"Do you think she could be in shock?" Jocelyn heard Hildy ask him. "Maybe we should have taken her to the hospital."

"The hospital is too far away," Clint said. "I'll call the doctor when we get inside."

"I don't need a doctor." Jocelyn managed to say halfway up the path to the A-frame house. "I just need to sit quietly for a while."

"We'll see," Clint said.

She nodded and let him hurry her up the path.

Once they were inside the house, Clint found dry clothes for Hildy and Jocelyn. Then he built a fire in the fireplace while they were changing. Jocelyn came out first wearing one of Clint's sweatshirts. She'd had to roll the sleeves up several turns, and the bottom hung down toward her knees. His black sweat pants puddled around her bare ankles. The way he looked at her, with his eyes shining as bright as the fire in the grate, made her blush and glance away.

"You need something on your feet. I'll get you some socks," he said and hurried out of the room.

Jocelyn sat down by the fire, wondering if she could look forward to another pair of stretched argyles like Hildy's. She had washed up in Clint's bathroom and removed what remained of DeDe's mud-sodden bandage. The blister beneath it was in pretty good shape. At least, it didn't hurt now. Jocelyn found a Band-Aid in Clint's medicine cabinet to cover the area awhile longer. When Clint returned with a pair of white cotton athletic socks, Jocelyn agreed that her blister was healed enough for her to wear something over it. Besides, her toes were cold, like the rest of her body had been before she sat down close to the fire.

She reached out to take the socks from Clint, but he had already gotten down on one knee in front of her.

"I'm the second person you've had at your feet today. Do you make a habit of this kind of thing?"

Jocelyn knew he was referring to DeDe's nursing the blister. He was also trying to cheer her somber mood. Unfortunately, his comment only made her sigh. Had it actually been today that she was at the Mapes place? Technically speaking, it was well after midnight now, so that had happened yesterday. Still, she hadn't been to sleep yet, so she might count it as all happening in a single day—the most eventful day she had lived or hoped she would ever live.

The oversupply of adrenaline that had made her restless back at Hildy's trailer was all used up long ago. Jocelyn would have loved to lean back on Clint's deep-cushioned couch, cover herself with the Indian blanket that was folded nearby and fall immediately into sleep.

Firelight danced on the soft finish of the wide-planked floor and was reflected in the opposite wall, which was glass from floor to cathedral ceiling. She had seen enough of Clint's house to know it was lovely and cozy, as well. She told herself she mustn't get too comfortable. She would sleep at Hildy's trailer tonight as originally planned. Meanwhile, there were things Jocelyn had to find out before she could go to sleep anywhere.

Clint had put on both of her socks, slipping the right one gently over the Band-Aid on her heel. Hildy hadn't returned from changing her clothes, and Jocelyn was beginning to be curious about that. She would go looking for her older friend in a little while. But first, Jocelyn had other questions that needed answers.

"What were you doing out at that quarry tonight?" she asked.

Clint had sat down on a large brown-suede-covered cushion on the floor in front of the fire. He was gazing into the flames, which reminded Jocelyn of the night they met. He had been staring into her fire then. He turned toward her, and, like that first night, the light from the flames was too subdued to let her see the expression in his deep-set eyes. She would have liked to be able to read his face, but she had to settle for listening for clues in his voice.

"I know this probably won't go down very well with you since you're such an independent type," he said. "But I was watching Hildy's trailer when you left it."

"Why were you doing that?"

"After that break-in at your trailer, I thought somebody should keep an eye on things for a while in case the creep decided to come back. Since the police weren't going to do it, I elected myself."

He might be telling the truth, but then again he might not.

"Why did you follow us?" she asked.

"I saw you walk back down to your trailer and go inside for a minute."

"I was picking up my car keys."

"While you were in there, Sonny Shannon drove off. Then you two pulled out next. There isn't much traffic around the campground late at night. I thought you might be following him and get yourself in trouble. So I decided to tag along, too."

"I didn't see anybody else leaving when we did, but why would following Sonny get me into trouble?"

"Is that Sonny Shannon you're talking about?" Hildy was on the stairs leading down from Clint's loft bedroom. From the tangled disarray of her hair and the way she was rubbing her eyes, it looked as if she might have fallen asleep up there. "He could be trouble for anybody."

"We weren't really talking about Sonny," Jocelyn said. She was trying not to sound too annoyed by Hildy's interruption when there were still so many questions that Clint needed to answer. "Clint was just telling me about how he had us under surveillance tonight."

"Is that right?" Hildy asked, coming down the stairs the rest of the way and watching Clint suspiciously.

"I thought that whoever let himself into Jocelyn's trailer without being asked might try it again," he said.

"Wouldn't that be unusual? A thief striking the same place twice in one night?" Hildy asked.

"Jocelyn's visitor wasn't a thief. There wasn't anything taken. He wasn't a vandal, either. There wasn't enough damage for that," Clint said. "So he had to be looking for something. I don't think he found it."

"What makes you say that?" Hildy asked, obviously relishing her role as interrogator.

"The hanging flowerpot," he said. "It doesn't make sense to me that he would check that before going into the trailer. It's too much of a long shot as a possible hiding place. My guess is that he checked it on the way out, which means he hadn't found anything inside."

"Maybe he found what he was looking for in the flowerpot, after all," Hildy said.

"Maybe" was all Clint answered.

"That explains why you would be watching my trailer," Jocelyn said. "But you told me you were watching Hildy's, too."

"I was doing both, or trying to."

"You were running back and forth between Hildy's place and mine in the middle of the night?"

"Something like that."

Jocelyn shook her head. "Sounds like bizarre behavior to me."

"Everything about tonight was bizarre," Hildy said. "Especially what happened at the quarry."

Jocelyn stood up fast and stepped between Clint and Hildy. "We just got caught in the rain, and I lost my flashlight and panicked a little."

She made a grimace at Hildy that was a signal for her to keep quiet. Jocelyn hoped there was enough light from the fire for Hildy to see. There must have been because she sat down on the couch and didn't say anything more.

"I think we should be going now," Jocelyn said, looking from Hildy to Clint.

"You could stay here," he said. "I have plenty of room."

"No, I wouldn't want to do that," Jocelyn said, looking down at the socks on her feet and wondering what she would put on over them. Footwear certainly seemed to have become a problem for her lately.

Clint must have noticed her downward glance. "I think I have a pair of boots you can wear," he said. He opened a door on the other side of the stairway. "By the way, what were you doing in that quarry, anyway?"

"Hildy wanted to show me her excavation."

"In a rainstorm?" he asked.

"Something like that," Jocelyn parroted what he had said a moment or two ago.

"Sounds like bizarre behavior to me."

She almost smiled but didn't. "Are those boots you mentioned in there?" She gestured toward the closet he had opened.

He rummaged inside then pulled out a pair of olive green rubber knee highs that looked way too small for him. "These belonged to my brother," he said.

Jocelyn heard something in his voice that time. It was the same subdued tone he always used when he mentioned Patrick. She remembered what Sonny had said about the circumstances of Patrick's death and how Clint could not accept what everybody else assumed to be the truth. His brother's loss was still a painful subject for Clint. Jocelyn felt a wave of compassion for him pass over her so strong that she almost didn't ask the other question she'd had in mind ever since she first started thinking clearly again after her unsettling experience at the quarry.

She steeled herself and asked anyway. "Have you ever played a musical instrument?"

"What was that?"

Jocelyn had put on the boots, and Clint was handing her a hunting jacket when he asked that.

"I know it sounds silly, but it's something I've been wondering about."

Jocelyn smiled warmly at Clint, and that must have done the trick.

"I played sax in my high school dance band," he said.

"Thanks," she said, shrugging into the hunting jacket while Hildy watched the two of them with a quizzical look on her face.

"I'll bring your car over to the campground in the morning," Clint said.

Jocelyn had been on her way toward the door. She spun around toward him. "No, don't do that," she said so sharply that Hildy seemed startled. "I would really rather drive my car myself," Jocelyn added more calmly.

She didn't say more or wait for Clint to answer. She walked to the door, opened it, pulled up the collar of the hunting jacket and stepped out into the rain. Her hair had dried in the heat from the fireplace. Now it was getting wet again, but she didn't notice. She could hardly notice anything, her heart was aching so. This evening she had recognized the truth she had not wanted to admit to herself. She was falling in love with Clint Conti, and she didn't seem to be able to stop herself.

She had been lost in that thought, like a child lost in a maze, until Clint said the word "saxophone." Now another equally agonizing thought had overtaken her. She was thinking about how the principles of fingering and playing the saxophone and the flute were basically the same. Philip had told her that. He had also told her that someone who could play one of those instruments could often play the other. She wondered how many instruments Clint could play—not counting the strings of her breaking heart.

Chapter Thirteen

When Jocelyn awoke the next day, she could tell there was not much left of the morning. Hildy's trailer was older and not as well insulated as Jocelyn's. The bedroom took in the heat of the heightening sun and had no way of releasing it again. The tiny windows were open but hardly adequate to cool the room. It was probably the heat that had wakened Jocelyn. She felt so tired still that if it hadn't been for the discomfort, she might have closed her eyes again and slept the clock around.

She pulled back the sheet that had been covering her and saw something slide onto the floor. She peered over the side of the bed to see what it might be. She recognized what looked like a native American talisman of some kind—blades of dried grasses, a bird's feather and a small pouch that was full to bulging, all lashed together by a strip of rawhide. She guessed that Hildy had made this and left it on the bed for a reason. She had meant to protect Jocelyn in some way. She was sure of it. Though generally skeptical about such mumbo jumbo, Jocelyn was happy to have some magic on her side after the events of last night.

Hildy had apparently been busy with more mundane tasks, as well. Folded over the end of the bed were a blue short-cropped T-shirt, a pair of white deck pants and clean underwear. Jocelyn's white canvas flats were on the floor near the other clothes, which must have been brought here from Jocelyn's trailer earlier this morning. It was the perfect outfit for a warm summer day of outdoor fun. Unfortunately, Jocelyn doubted that was what lay ahead of her. The hangover from yesterday's events weighed on her as heavily as if she had spent the night guzzling what north country folk referred to as bad brown whiskey. Heat or not, she was truly tempted to crawl back into bed and sleep the clock around, after all.

Instead, she pulled on Hildy's robe, grabbed a towel, some shampoo and the clothes and plodded over to one of the campground shower rooms. Hildy had left a note that her shower wasn't working. She was using it to store specimens. Jocelyn wasn't accustomed to the public facilities, but they turned out to be a blessing in disguise. The water burst from the shower head much more sharply and at a considerably lower temperature than would have been the case in Jocelyn's very modern little bathroom.

She jumped when the needles of chill water first hit her body. Then those needles began working their own kind of magic, waking her up a bit more with each wet barrage. She let herself be prodded back to life by the water. She soaped her body slick and sweet smelling all over. As the water cascaded over her, carrying the perfumed lather between her breasts, across her belly and down her thighs, Jocelyn imagined the strains and stresses of these past harrowing days washing away. The white foam gurgled out of sight and her troubles out of mind down the round grate in the shower-stall floor. Still, she knew that this was only a temporary respite. As she worked shampoo into a thick lather through her hair, she was grateful for any relief at all, no matter how short-lived.

Back in Hildy's trailer, Jocelyn rummaged through the medicine cabinet for a Band-Aid to protect her heel, which was actually nearly back to normal already. DeDe's home remedy had worked like a charm. Jocelyn recalled how efficiently yet tenderly DeDe had ministered to Jocelyn's blistered foot and how trustingly she had let that happen. Surprising behavior between women who had been rivals for the same man.

Jocelyn didn't like being reminded of Philip's duplicity and all the trouble that went with it. For an instant, she indulged herself in an impossible wish—that she would walk out of Hildy's trailer cum research lab into a world that was free of complications and maddening doubts. The fantasy took on its own momentum and clicked her make-believe move another frame forward. Just beyond that imaginary threshold into a less frustrating world stood Clint Conti. He was tall and handsome as always, and the shimmering sunlight of this idyllic scene seemed to radiate out of him as well as around him.

Jocelyn slammed the medicine-cabinet door closed a bit too vehemently. She gasped at herself, grateful she hadn't broken the mirror. She checked inside to make sure the contents were undamaged. Then she began looking for a hair dryer. Her hair could be finger combed and left to dry naturally. Jocelyn was really more in need of distractions than she was of a hair dryer. Anything would do that could keep her from thinking about Clint, the man who was the source of her most worrisome doubts and confusions.

She did find a hair dryer in the cupboard under the bathroom sink. She plugged it in and darted it impatiently back and forth around her head, too agitated to aim the nozzle long enough in any single direction to do much good. She tried to concentrate on the image of Hildy using this thing to blow her wild hair into even more chaos. Ordinarily, Jocelyn would have found some amusement in that. Today, she couldn't even manage to crack a smile.

WHAT JOCELYN FOUND at her own trailer did cheer her up some. Hildy and the Delaneys and Jocelyn's two sets of neighbors from beyond the tree line had gotten together earlier to clean up her trailer while she was still sleeping. They all agreed that Jocelyn had been through enough already and deserved to rest. By the time she showed up, the place was back to normal once again. Even the impatiens had been repotted and hung in its planter over the deck, with all trace of last night's spilled soil swept away and gone. The spot in the living room where the flower vase water had been dumped on the carpet was scrubbed clean with only a fading damp mark against the blue as evidence of last night's upheaval. Someone had even thought to fetch the Lincoln from the quarry.

Jocelyn was so thankful that she hardly knew what to say. She had been dreading the task of cleaning up the mess some anonymous intruder had made of her private place. She bit back tears of gratitude and relief. She remembered wondering whether she would make friends here this summer. Thanks to some very unusual circumstances, she had. She hoped that recalling the warmth of new friends would get her through the anxiety, and the fearsomeness, of what she had to do next.

JOCELYN REMEMBERED the route to Clint's house. Hildy had offered to come along and had looked worried when Jocelyn insisted on driving off alone and deliberately failed to mention where she was going. This was something she had to do on her own. Besides, as much of a free spirit as Hildy was, she might not approve of breaking and entering.

Jocelyn was relieved and surprised to find that Clint wasn't at home. The way things had been going lately she couldn't help but be astonished when anything at all proceeded as she hoped it would. To add to today's streak of welcome luck, the sliding door in the glass wall at the rear of Clint's A-frame was unlocked. That was typical of north country people, at least the ones who lived this far into the rural areas. The front door might be latched, but there was very likely to be an unsecured door out back or a window somewhere that nobody had thought to close. Jocelyn whispered an only slightly guilty prayer of thanks as she pushed the door open and slipped inside.

The air was redolent of last night's blaze in the fireplace, where the ashes now lay cold and gray around the charred carcass of a log. Jocelyn had already decided to go about her search systematically, beginning with the upstairs loft. She climbed the wooden staircase that had been set into the exposed fieldstone chimney that ran upward from the fireplace through Clint's bedroom where it opened into a smaller fireplace facing the bed. She did her best not to admire how carefully everything had been designed for both efficiency and comfort. She wished she could deny how beautiful the result was, as well. She didn't want to be appreciating anything about Clint's life right now—perhaps not ever.

Jocelyn avoided looking at the king-size bed and the small fireplace facing it. She was proud of herself for only briefly indulging in a fantasy of herself and Clint lying there together side by side.

She forced herself to focus on rummaging through first the bedside table drawers then the dresser and a trunk at the bottom of the bed. There was another photograph of Clint and Patrick on the fireplace mantel. The picture was set in an antique silver frame, which contrasted noticeably with the other more ruggedly masculine objects in the room. Jocelyn understood that this special frame symbolized the special relationship there had been between these two brothers. She was also fairly certain the photo had not been so elaborately framed until after Patrick's death. It was the closest thing to a shrine that a man like Clint would allow himself. She fought down the wave of compassion for Clint that threatened to engulf her and continued her search.

There was nothing in the loft that could help her. She went back downstairs, thinking about how she was invading Clint's private place as surely as last night's intruder at her trailer had invaded hers. There was no point in telling herself her behavior was justified. Whoever broke into her trailer had probably thought that he or she was justified, too. She was no better than that person had been. Wrong was wrong. She had known that when she decided to come here today. She had traded her integrity for the opportunity to seek some answers to the mounting questions and doubts she had about Clint's real reasons for becoming so suddenly and intensely involved in her life. She still desperately needed answers and so proceeded to search the ground floor of the house.

The closet where Clint had found boots for her last night was full of interesting things—fishing tackle, a hunting rifle, snowshoes, even a butterfly net—but nothing that told Jocelyn what she needed to know. She moved on toward the office area in the back corner of the house, checking the magazine rack and drawers in tables along the way but to no avail. She had saved the office space till last on purpose, though that didn't necessarily constitute good logic. Since the office was the most likely room to produce pay dirt, she might preferably have begun her search here. A dispassionate observer might have concluded that she didn't really want to find out anything incriminating about Clint and was, therefore, sabotaging the effort. Jocelyn didn't let herself believe that could be true.

She did let herself take a moment to admire the view from Clint's office windows. The wall of glass continued along the back wall and around the corner to the side. Clint had set his desk beneath the angle of the A-frame corner, facing the outdoors. He had built his house on the banks of one of the small woodland lakes that dotted the north country. There were trees along the banks on all sides of the lake except for the area Clint had cleared below the deck for a dock and a narrow swimming beach.

A single oak grew at the edge of the water with one stocky branch nearly as thick as the trunk angling out over the swimming place. A sturdy plaited rope with a large knot toward the bottom had been tied to the branch and trailed down almost to the surface of the lake. Jocelyn could imagine Clint swinging on that rope, outward from the tree, then letting go and dropping into the water with a quick splash. It was a thing you did in lovely country places like this one, where some of the natural, exuberant joys of being a boy could be felt all over again by a grown man.

Jocelyn turned back to the desk, away from the beautiful view of the sun-dappled lake and the entrancing vision of Clint's soaring outward over sparkling water on the rope of her imagination. She had pulled out the lap drawer of the desk and was picking through a pile of utility bills when she heard the sound of a truck engine. She pushed the desk drawer shut with shaking fingers, but didn't panic or bolt for the door. There wouldn't be any way for her to get out of here and off in the Lincoln without Clint seeing or hearing her. She had realized that when she first planned this excursion. She had come up with a much better plan for covering her tracks than running away.

Earlier, on the way into the house, Jocelyn had set her pile of Clint's borrowed clothes on the couch in front of the fireplace. She was standing next to that clothing when Clint arrived. He stepped through the doorway, and her heart was racing. She told herself that was because of the lie she was about to tell. In the instant it took for him to enter the room, she had time to wonder when her heart had last raced over anything more personal than a fast set of tennis. It must have been before Philip. One of the major reasons she had chosen Philip was that he calmed things down rather than stirred them up.

Had she ever felt comfortable with emotional intensity? Had growing up with her mother made Jocelyn gun-shy of chaos, emotional or otherwise? She asked herself these questions in the seconds it took Clint to cross from the door to the couch and look down at her quizzically.

"This is a nice surprise," he said.

"I stopped over to return your things." She gestured at the pile of clothes on the couch and the boots on the floor next to them. "When you weren't here I thought I should leave them inside."

"Thanks." Clint nodded, not appearing to suspect that her words were anything but the truth.

Jocelyn felt suddenly awkward. She wasn't as comfortable with the role of intruder and deceiver as she needed to be. If she stuck around here much longer, her nervousness would be sure to give her away.

"I'd better be going," she said, and moved to step past him toward the door.

Clint touched her arm just firmly enough to make her pause for a moment.

"I was just out at Tranquility," he said. "Two sheriff's deputies were at your trailer looking for you."

"Did they say what they wanted?"

"They only said they wanted to talk to you. They wouldn't get into it any further than that. Maybe you should drive over to the sheriff's office in Lowville and see if you can find out what's up."

"Yes, I think I'd better do that," Jocelyn said thoughtfully.

"Would you like me to come with you for moral support?"

"What?" Jocelyn had been so preoccupied that she didn't grasp the meaning of Clint's words for a moment.

"I would like to tag along if you'd let me," he said.

She couldn't think of any compelling reason to refuse. Her doubts about Clint could be groundless. She hadn't found anything concrete except a couple of troubling photographs, and there might very well be a logical explanation for those. Besides, the truth was that she didn't want to go to the sheriff's office on her own, especially since she strongly suspected that whatever they had to tell her wouldn't be good news.

"Now that you mention it," she said, "I wouldn't mind the company." And she meant it.

JOCELYN HAD NEVER been inside the Lewis County Sheriff's Station. She might have imagined that in a small town, there would be a cozy feel to the place. She would have been wrong. Harsh fluorescent lighting and grimy green paint prevailed, just like on any television cop show set. She hadn't really noticed last evening, but the sheriff's deputy looked like something out of central casting himself. His uniform shirt had been pressed with such military precision that you might have cut your finger on the sharp creases in the sleeves. Even his belt looked as if it must have been spit polished. He wasn't wearing the obligatory dark aviator-style glasses she would have expected on such a front-and-center kind of guy, but Jocelyn would have bet money he had a pair lying around somewhere waiting to be slapped onto the bridge of his once-broken nose.

"Deputy Roemer," he said. "We met last night, ma'am."

"I remember."

Jocelyn hadn't caught his name at the time. In fact, she didn't recall anyone ever mentioning it. Her recollections of last night were mostly isolated scenes or glimpses of scenes—the wildflowers strewn over her carpet, wind and rain whipping across the quarry floor, a pair of rubber boots in Clint's hand. She was certain it would all come together in a coherent whole eventually. For now, she would prefer that no one knew how disjointed her memories really were or how distraught she had been at the time. She would rather be seen as in control. For that reason, she deliberately set about being extra observant of everything that was happening around her.

The first thing she noticed was that Deputy Roemer was no longer as uninterested in her situation as he had been the night before, when he could hardly wait to get away from the scene of what he obviously assumed to be a case of random teenage vandalism. Today, he ushered her into a separate office and left instructions to hold any calls he might receive while he was speaking with her. Jocelyn wondered why she suddenly merited such priority treatment.

She also noticed some tension between the deputy and Clint, who had followed her into the station and stood off to the side. The two men had nodded at each other, but that was all. When the deputy invited Jocelyn to accompany him into the back office, he made clear that she should come alone. She told Clint that he could go on home since she had driven her own car here, but he said he would stick around. Deputy Roemer didn't look too pleased about that. Jocelyn wondered if their behavior had something to do with Clint's brother, Patrick.

Once inside the cramped office, however, Jocelyn forgot all about Patrick Conti. The desktop was covered with faxes. They had been divided into two groups of separate piles. Each pile had something set on top of it—a stapler, a paper-clip holder, a letter opener—to keep the slick paper pages from curling. At the head of each of the two groups of faxes was a manila file folder. Jocelyn leaned over the desk to read what was written on the identification tab of each folder. Even reading upside down, she could easily decipher that one said "Philip Wald" and the other said "Reggie Williams."

The deputy invited her to sit down but didn't give her time to settle herself before dropping his bombshell.

"It appears that your late husband was living a double life," he said.

Later on, Jocelyn would guess that Roemer intended this abrupt approach to shock some reaction out of her that might indicate how much she really had known about Philip's alternative identity. At the moment, she wasn't able to be quite that analytical. The most she could deduce was that the deputy must be referring to something more than an extramarital affair. A domestic matter wasn't likely to generate this amount of paperwork or such serious attention, either. She did her best to maintain the fiction of being in control and waited for him to continue.

"Have you ever heard of a company called North Country Wash and Dry?" he asked.

Jocelyn thought for a moment, both about an answer and why such an odd question was being asked. "I don't believe so," she said. "Does that company have something to do with Philip?"

"I'd say it does. He owned it." Deputy Roemer tapped one of the piles of faxes. "Or, according to these, Reggie Williams did."

"Philip never mentioned anything like that to me. What kind of business was it?"

"A chain of coin-operated laundries," he said, watching her closely. "They're all over the area. Lewis, Jefferson, even St. Lawrence counties. Laundry seems to have been a lucrative business for your husband."

"I see," Jocelyn said, though she didn't really see at all.

"And you knew nothing at all about this company?"

"Nothing at all." Jocelyn felt her in-control facade in danger of slipping.

"Do you know anything about these?" Roemer poked his finger at another pile of faxes, also on the Reggie Williams side of his desk.

"What are they?"

Jocelyn leaned forward to get a better view of what he was pointing at, but he picked up the pages before she could get a look at them.

"Bank accounts," he said, brandishing the pages in front of her for a second or two then pulling them away. "Reggie Williams had money in banks all over northern New York, at least one in every town where one of his laundries was operating."

The deputy sat down in the worn leather chair behind the desk and stared at her while tapping the sheaf of faxes against the sharp pants crease along his thigh.

"What do you think about that?" he asked.

Jocelyn let out a deep sigh. She had absolutely no idea what she thought about anything at the moment, as she felt the remnants of her pretense at control evaporate.

JOCELYN HAD TO ADMIT she was relieved to find Clint still waiting when she finally left the police station. He was sitting in his truck, which he had parked next to the

Lincoln in the lot. He jumped down from the cab when he saw her and hurried to meet her.

"What happened?" he asked.

"I think I'm under suspicion of something, but I'm not sure what. I don't think they're sure about that, either."

"Maybe you should have had a lawyer in there with you."

"That occurred to me, but I don't think it would have made much difference. Deputy Roemer kept asking me the same questions over and over. I kept answering that I didn't know anything, and I'm sad to say that was the truth."

Jocelyn yanked open the door to the Lincoln. She was feeling a combination of discouragement and anger. Several times back there in the sheriff's office, she had wanted to slap the deputy very hard across the face or rip the buttons off his perfect shirtfront. She understood that it wasn't really him she was angry with. It was this crazy circumstance she found herself in that had her so infuriated. She needed to know the truth he had to tell her, but she didn't want to hear it, either. What she did want was to turn this oversize car south and race back to the house on Genessee Street as fast as she could go. She would close herself up once again inside that big house and not let anyone in no matter who they might be. Unfortunately, she had already broken the seal on that particular sanctum. Her newfound self was not about to let her hide out any longer, even if the good deputy would have allowed it.

"How about letting me cook you supper," Clint said.

Jocelyn was surprised to hear him mention suppertime. She hadn't realized how late it was. The afternoon was fading away. The sun had taken on the more golden tone of approaching evening. She had been in the sheriff's office a long time.

"I don't know if I could eat anything," she began to say.

"There's more to it than that," Clint said quickly. He took her arm to keep her from getting into her car before he could have his say. "I have to talk to you about some things. Things I probably should have told you before, but I didn't want to scare you away."

Jocelyn could hear the earnestness in his tone. "Are these things about Philip?"

Clint hesitated. "They're about me," he said.

He dropped her arm and stared down at her. She certainly would like to have some of her questions about him cleared up.

"My place or yours?" she asked, marveling that she could sound so casual.

"Mine," he said. "In my kitchen I'm like a captain on his ship."

Jocelyn nodded as she got into the Lincoln. She had no doubt that Clint was the captain in all rooms of his house—especially the one she didn't feel up to thinking about right now.

CLINT PROVED TRUE to his word. He was a masterful cook, though a simple one. Meat, potatoes and salad— real man's food—but well seasoned and cooked just right. Jocelyn had been wrong about not being able to eat anything. She polished off a steak and baked potato and a bowl of fresh garden greens with vegetables swimming in Roquefort dressing. When Clint asked what her last full meal had been, all she could remember were the charred hot dogs on Sonny's grill. She hadn't been in the frame of mind to think much about food since then.

Clint laid a fire in the fireplace and brought in mugs of steaming coffee. Then he finally broached the subject he had brought her here to discuss.

"My brother Patrick meant everything to me," he said. "He knew me better than anybody has ever known me. Better than I've ever let anybody know me."

Clint was staring into the fire as he spoke. Jocelyn didn't interrupt. She watched his profile and let him talk.

"I was that close to Patrick, too. He told me everything. Even when I moved away, we called each other and he would come to visit me. He knew what was in my heart, and I knew what was in his. One thing I am absolutely certain of. He never could have done anything dishonest or illegal. He never could have done what they accused him of." Clint paused and looked over at her. "I assume somebody has told you that he was suspended from the police force for suspicion of being involved in a crooked money deal."

"I had heard about the suspension," Jocelyn said quietly.

"I figured you would have. A good juicy story like that can't help but get passed around a small place like this. It happened a year ago, and it's still hot gossip."

The bitterness in his tone kept Jocelyn from responding.

"Well, he didn't do it." Clint slapped his mug down so hard on the floor that coffee splashed out. "And he didn't kill himself, either. He would have agreed with that big ape at the flea market yesterday. Suicide's the coward's way out, and Patrick was no coward."

"Then what do you think did happen to him?" Jocelyn couldn't help but ask, despite the voice of common sense that told her to keep silent and let him blow off some steam.

Clint bolted up from the sofa where he had been sitting next to her. He began pacing back and forth in front of the fireplace, grinding his clenched fist into his palm.

"I don't know," he said. "I don't know what happened."

His anguish was more than Jocelyn could bear. She stood up and stepped in front of him. "You mustn't torment yourself like this. What good can it do?"

"Good?" he asked, grabbing her shoulders in his strong, square hands. "You are the only good thing that has happened to me in this whole long, lousy year."

He was crying out to her, and Jocelyn's heart filled in response. She knew he was going to kiss her. She didn't move to stop him. She expected the same kind of hard embrace as last night at the pavilion, but that was not how it began.

Clint slipped his arms around her so gently that she sensed more than felt them there. He enfolded her to him, and when his full lips covered hers he breathed her into him, as well. She moaned deep in her throat, and his moan answered hers. They were crying out to each other now, out of their mutual need for succor and relief—and love.

That word was in Jocelyn's mind, but it had come from her heart. Her only coherent thought was that she had never felt this way before, so filled up with tenderness and warmth and caring. She was not afraid.

There could be no fear of something so obviously right and good.

Jocelyn moved her hands up his arms, feeling the silken strands of dark gold hairs and the taut sinews beneath them. She touched the hard certainty of his biceps and knew he could crush her in an instant. Instead, he continued to cradle her in his arms as if she were all of a sudden too fragile to manhandle as he had done last night.

All the while their lips played over one another, tasting and feeling and learning each other's softness in a long, slow moment of discovery. Their tongues touched, and in that instant a transformation began. The tip of his tongue cleft her suddenly, wonderfully open, like a blade of desire. The hot apex of that blade shot downward through her and burst into fire in her loins. She had been a married woman for most of her adult life, but here and now she was a virgin hungering to be taken for the first time by her one true and only lover for whom she had waited what seemed like an eternity of emptiness and longing.

Jocelyn ran her fingers hard along the brawny breadth of his shoulders. She felt the power there and took it into herself. She clasped his face in her hands and pulled his mouth away from hers with such strength that his eyes opened and he looked down at her with surprise.

"I want you," she said in a voice that rose from a place in her never heard from before. "I want you now."

Clint gazed into her eyes for only a moment. There passed between them a charge of such shock and intensity that she knew without a doubt he must feel it, too. His arm slipped behind her knees, and he lifted her

with ease. He continued to gaze into her eyes as he
carried her to the staircase and began to climb.

His lips were parted, but he didn't speak, at least not
in words. There was sound inside him nonetheless, and
Jocelyn heard it. His breathing was so deep and ragged that it echoed in his chest. She could feel the resonance of it against her body. She turned toward him
and touched her own feverish lips to the throbbing
warmth of his throat.

"My love," he whispered down at her and hurried
faster up the remaining stairs.

They might have stumbled, but Jocelyn knew they
would not. There would be no stumbling tonight. No
awkwardness. No sense of being anything but each
other's destiny. They would be naked together for the
first time. Yet, they would recognize each other at
once, as the soul recognizes its mate. He would enter
into her, and at last she would be whole.

This aching within her now, as he set her on the bed
and fell down beside her, was the exquisite pain of
knowing she was only moments from opening her body
to him in a way she had never done for any man before. Her voice pleaded for those moments to pass
quickly. Her mouth drank him in, and her thirst became greater still. Her fingers caressed and explored,
greedy to fondle and stroke every inch of him.

He was touching her, as well, and suckling her with
his mouth as the clothes between them seemed to fly
away. She was so lost in the sensations of experiencing
him through her lips and fingertips that she was not
specifically aware of what he was doing to her breasts
and belly and thighs. She only felt the flame within her
grow to a pulsing hotness that spread through her,

making her body a torrid zone desperate for the respite of a storm.

The muscles at the very heart of this consuming fire
began to move in a way they had never moved before.
When she felt him at the entrance of her, the pulsating
movement quickened.

He came into her, and she screamed. She couldn't
help it. He had thrust through the long years of lone-
liness and yearning she had never dared acknowledge.
He had ripped through the wall that had kept her
sealed off from the secret of what love could truly be.
And Jocelyn, as she arched and thrust with urgency
equal to his, had become fully a woman at last.

Chapter Fourteen

It was barely morning. Early dawn light crept through the cedar blinds of the peaked window above Clint's bed.

He must have had those blinds specially made, thought Jocelyn.

The window had been designed into the apex of the A-frame. The blinds were a perfect fit, like everything else in his house. The textures, the colors, the pieces of pottery and colored glasswork placed here and there all attested to the care he had taken with each detail. Those details were subtle, yet to Jocelyn they spoke loudly of the kind of man who lay beside her now. What this place said about Clint Conti warmed Jocelyn like rays of noonday sun.

She rose on one elbow, moving quietly in order not to wake him. Pale morning light found the auburn glints among the blackness of his hair. His face was turned slightly away from her. His arm was flung above his head. The dark, silken strands beneath his arm were displayed. She longed to touch them but knew that would waken him for sure.

She smiled at herself. Before this moment, she could never have imagined herself rhapsodizing over a man's underarm hair. That simply was not the kind of thing she did. She had always been too practical for such girlish gushing. Now, she could feel that part of herself changing. She was in the thrall of a breathless crush, or maybe even more. She tested the newness of that, at the full center of her heart, and it felt good.

She was also newly aware of the womanly parts of her, freshly alive and sensitive to the touch of the sheets and feeling well used from their long and intense lovemaking the night before. Jocelyn understood that she had been slumbering and at last she was awake, to much more than the rays of the morning sun.

A faded navy blue terry-cloth robe hung on a wooden wall peg nearby. She slipped quietly out of bed and put it on. The smooth worn fabric felt familiar along her skin, as familiar as its scent of Clint had become in only these few hours. The wood floors were chilly beneath her bare feet. She pulled on the white canvas flats she could not recall discarding at the foot of Clint's bed, then tiptoed carefully down the stairs with no particular destination in mind. She felt too alive and happy to lie still in bed any longer, and Clint's house seemed so much like home to her that it was as natural to her to move freely here as it would be in a place of her own.

Like yesterday, the pungency of a fireplace blaze remained in the air. Two half-empty coffee mugs were on the floor in front of the couch. The pile of neatly folded clothes remained where she had set them down after first arriving yesterday afternoon. At the time, returning those clothes had been her subterfuge for coming here. She marveled that she had needed any excuse for being where she now knew she so naturally belonged. She took the mugs into the kitchen and rinsed them in the sink, which was still filled with dirty dishes from last night's meal. She would have washed them, but the noise might waken Clint in the bedroom loft above.

She wandered back through the living room into Clint's office to gaze through the glass wall beyond his desk. A layer of mist hovered over the lake, drifting with the breeze and thinning in the pale sunlight that would soon evaporate it altogether. A mallard duck glided along the surface just beneath the mist. His jewel green head gleamed in the sun as he moved through the water without appearing to move at all. His webbed feet might be paddling furiously beneath him, but they were out of sight. To Jocelyn's eyes he was the picture of serenity, as easily at peace as she was herself on this glorious morning.

Jocelyn's glance wandered to Clint's desk, and she was struck by a twinge of guilty memory. She had been rifling through this desk yesterday afternoon when Clint arrived, almost catching her in the act. She didn't feel at all good about that now. Still, she could not keep other memories from invading her reverie, as well. She had been making that search for a reason. She had questions about Clint and his behavior. The events of last night might have warmed her heart toward him, but those questions remained unanswered. They nagged at her now and threatened her state of bliss with their persistence.

She listened. There was no sound from the loft. Clint must still be sleeping. She eased the desk drawers open very carefully, one after the other, searching each thoroughly and finding nothing. She approached the final drawer, withholding her relief to the last but allowing herself the hope that she would find nothing to chill the glow that Clint's touch had brought to her body and soul.

The first clutch of dread began when that final drawer didn't slide out as easily as the others had. There was nothing inside to cause her alarm, but she knew she had to look underneath. She pulled the drawer toward her as far as it would come then felt its underside. She did not want to find the manila envelope attached with masking tape to the bottom of the drawer. She was even more reluctant to pull it free and open it. Unfortunately, her suspicions wouldn't let her do otherwise.

She vaguely recognized the type of document she found inside. It was a copy of what is generally referred to as a "DBA," the official application for a company "Doing Business As" a particular name. The name on this document was agonizingly familiar to Jocelyn. The piece of paper Clint had hidden away in a secret corner of his desk was the DBA for a company entitled North Country Wash and Dry, and it was signed by Reggie Williams in her late husband's very recognizable hand.

Jocelyn's own hands were shaking so hard that she could barely get the paper back into its envelope. She retaped it too hastily beneath the drawer. If Clint examined the tape, he would probably be able to tell it had been disturbed. Jocelyn could not stop to fix it now. She had to get out of here. Every second she remained was more torturous than the last. She was careful not to make any noise sliding the drawer back into the desk. She must not let Clint wake up and find her before she could make her escape. Seeing him again would be too much pain for her to bear.

She tiptoed across the room and dropped his robe to the floor. She pulled on the sweatshirt and jogging pants from the neatly folded pile near the couch. The next to the last thing she wanted right now was to be wearing his clothes, but the *last* thing she wanted right now was to go back upstairs to get her own. She slipped out the door, leaving it ajar behind her to avoid the sound of closing it. She got into her car, released the hand brake and let the car roll in neutral gear backward down the incline of Clint's driveway and into the road. She had to start the engine then, but she knew that even if he heard he would be too late to stop her from leaving this lovely place where her aching heart told her she must never return.

ALL THE WAY BACK to Tranquility, Jocelyn tormented herself. Should she tell Deputy Roemer about what she had found in Clint's desk? Was she tempted to do that because she wanted to betray him the way she felt he had betrayed her? Was she correct in her suspicion that the document she had found had something to do with his brother's death? If that were true, what could the connection be?

By the time she got to her trailer, she had wrestled herself into a disgruntled mood from those uncomfortable questions. She banged the door shut behind her, locked the latch and drew the drapes together tight so nobody could possibly see in. She was absolutely determined to be left alone. She didn't care how well-meaning anyone's attentions might be, she did not want those attentions now. She even went through the trailer grabbing up things her well-meaning neighbors had wrongly positioned yesterday while they were cleaning up in here.

"The cookie tin doesn't belong there," she muttered and slammed the black découpage-trimmed canister down in the spot where she usually kept it.

She was aware of how ill-tempered and unreasonable she was being. She was also aware of how far out of line this behavior was with her characteristic docile acceptance of things. Philip would be shocked if he could see her like this. Or perhaps he would just be amused.

"To hell with what Philip would be," she said.

She was looking around for something else to grab or shove around or kick when she heard Hildy's unmistakable voice approaching outside.

"Oh, no. Not now, Hildy," Jocelyn said, more disgruntled than ever.

She definitely did not want to talk to Hildy right now, but how could she avoid her? Jocelyn had parked the car right out front, so it was obvious she was home. Unless Hildy might think Jocelyn was off with Clint somewhere and they had taken his truck. Were such assumptions being made about the two of them? They had been seen together on a number of occasions by a number of people. Jocelyn had spent enough time in the north country to know how the gossip network operated. Yesterday she would have blushed to have her name linked with Clint's. She would have been secretly pleased. Today the thought of it plunged a dagger of pain into her heart.

She knelt on the dinette seat and lifted one slat of the venetian blind to peek through, but she could not see Hildy. Her familiar voice sounded again, more from the other side of the trailer this time. Jocelyn stepped across the narrow width of the room and peered, just as surreptitiously, through the venetian blind over the sink. Hildy was out there, all right, but it wasn't Jocelyn she was calling to. Sonny Shannon was leaning through the doorway of his trailer as Hildy bustled down the road toward him brandishing her fist and looking very agitated. Jocelyn cranked the window open a crack so she could hear more clearly.

"...and I want you to stop it right now!" Hildy was exclaiming.

"Stop what?" Sonny asked, grinning at her.

"Stop following me. Stop spying on me. Stop snooping around my dig site at the quarry."

"Look, Hildy. I don't want to get into a big hassle with you, but I don't even know what you're talking about."

Hildy picked up speed and was scrambling across Sonny's campsite. She came close to knocking over one of his already precarious support posts and bringing the awning down on her head. Sonny held his ground in the doorway as she barreled toward him.

"You know exactly what I am talking about," she said, waggling an accusatory finger at him. "You are the reason it has stopped coming around. I believe you have deliberately chased it away."

"Chased what away?"

"The spirit, of course. I was very close to making contact. Then you chased it away."

"Spirit?" Sonny was chuckling openly now. "You mean the ghosts and goblins kind of spirit?"

"That is precisely what I mean, as you very well know." Hildy had reached the steps of Sonny's trailer and was craning and bobbing at him with each word she spoke, like a frizzy-headed bird.

Sonny's chuckle had escalated to a full-blown laugh. "Hildy, I would never do anything to come between you and your goblins. Believe me."

"I would not believe you if you were standing on a stack of Bibles." Hildy lunged up the first of the two steps to Sonny's trailer. He pulled his head back inside and slammed the door before she could get to it. "You leave my spirit alone," she said, still waggling her finger. "You will be very sorry if you don't."

Jocelyn cranked the window shut fast and tight and let go of the venetian-blind slat. She would have laughed, if she hadn't felt so much like crying.

ALL JOCELYN WANTED was a way out of here. She would pack her things and drive back to Syracuse. As for Philip's alleged double life, she could hire somebody to look into whatever the police turned up. That person could chase down the bank accounts, tally up any outstanding bills and pay them, then pass on any legal loose ends there might be to a lawyer. She could find someone to do all of that for her, someone who would do it as a job, who wouldn't suffer with every revelation as if a fresh wound had been gouged into his soul.

She thought about what she would pack to leave, what she would leave behind. She would prefer to walk out, lock the door and take off. Unfortunately, the practical side of her still did exist. She knew there was more to leaving this trailer than that. At the very least, she had to clean out the refrigerator and turn off the gas. She had to batten down the windows and the blinds, and roll in the awning. If she wasn't planning to come back for a long time, she would have to trundle the outdoor furniture to the utility shed and lock it away in there.

Just thinking about what had to be done made Jocelyn feel weary. She sat down on the swivel chair next to the sliding glass doors. She understood that she was really making mental preparations for abandoning this place for good. She was noting to herself the things that would have to be done in order for this trailer to be put up for sale. She was even considering how low a price she would be willing to take just so she could be free of it sooner.

Again, she could hire somebody to handle the sale for her. They would put ads in the area papers, show potential buyers around, even negotiate the best deal. The Delaneys might be willing to do that for her. What the Delaneys could not do—or anybody else, either— would be to manage away the sadness Jocelyn would feel when this special place was no longer a part of her life. She was contemplating that sadness when a knock came on the glass doors so close to her that she jumped.

"Jocelyn, I want to talk to you. I know you're in there." It was Clint, and he sounded angry.

What did he have to be angry about? Jocelyn's indignation demanded to know.

"Let me in, Jocelyn. I'm not going to leave till you do."

She sighed. She should have made her escape from here when she first thought about it. Now she was stuck. She could hear the stubbornness in Clint's voice. If he said he intended to pound on her door until she let him in, then that was exactly what he would do. In deference to her neighbors who had already put up with more than enough disturbance because of her, Jocelyn stood up and unlatched the doors. She walked over to the couch and sat down. If Clint wanted the door actually opened for him, he would have to do it himself. He did.

He stepped inside the room. The space seemed to grow instantly cramped with him standing in it. He was too large for such compact quarters. Like a giant in a burrow, he didn't fit. The tension in him was obvious from his clenched fists and tight face muscles. If he had been less confined he might have started pacing. Instead, he shifted from one foot to the other and back again several times, as if his agitation required some kind of physical outlet to keep him from exploding on the spot.

Jocelyn tried not to pay attention to how handsome he looked with his jaw set square as granite and his green eyes flashing sparks. His hair had fallen over his forehead, and he raked it back so fiercely with his fingers that he might have left grooves on his scalp. It occurred to her that Clint angry was a frightening presence, but she was not afraid. She was ready for the confrontation he had obviously come here to have.

"I take it you found what you were looking for this morning," he said.

She did not answer. She wanted to find out exactly how much he knew before she said anything. She watched as he pulled a manila envelope from his jacket pocket and tossed it on the coffee table. She was pretty certain she recognized the envelope as the one she had found taped to the bottom drawer of his desk.

"You went to so much trouble to get it, you might as well have it," he said.

He turned away, and she thought he might leave. Her heart fluttered at the prospect of how empty the room would feel without his broad body filling it up. He stepped back and then to the side, as restless as a powerful beast in a locked cage. He spun around to face her again.

"You used me," he said. There was grief in his tone to match the anger.

"I used you? What about the way you've been using me? Weren't you trying to find out about Philip through me? Wasn't that the reason you kept coming around here in the first place?"

He looked at her for a moment. "In the first place, yes."

She debated saying something about how Patrick's death had to be tied into all of this in some way, but she still didn't want to reveal just how much she didn't know.

"And did you get what you wanted out of me?" she asked.

Clint stared at the blue carpet between his shifting feet. He shoved his hands into the pockets of his jeans.

"I didn't get what I thought I wanted," he said much more quietly. "I ended up wanting you so much I forgot what I had come here for."

"What exactly had you come here for?"

"To keep a promise I made at my brother's grave. Instead, I found myself falling in love with you. I even thought you might feel the same. Until this morning."

His body had stilled its trapped, restless motion for a moment. Now, it began again.

"What does all of this have to do with Philip?"

Jocelyn had decided to forget about the cat-and-mouse approach. She was feeling too upset to make it work, anyway. He said he was falling in love with her, but only until this morning. She knew that she felt the same. Only, however devastating this morning's discovery might have been, she had not been able to turn off her emotions the way she suspected he had.

"You really don't know anything about what your husband was up to, do you?"

"No, I don't. I don't know for sure that he was up to anything." Some residue of loyalty she felt she should have for a dead spouse made her say that.

"Didn't you wonder about his absences? Didn't the two of you ever talk to each other? Weren't you curious about where all his money came from?"

"What went on between myself and my husband is not your business." Her indignation was fueled by shame. Clint's accusing questions were way too close to the truth for comfort.

"It doesn't look like you made it much of your business either. In the beginning, I figured you had at least to have guessed some of what your husband was into. Now I really believe he managed to keep you completely in the dark, and he managed it because that was the way you wanted it. You wanted to hide inside your comfortable life and not be disturbed by the nastiness that was right smack on your doorstep."

"What exactly was my husband into?" Jocelyn asked very calmly, letting Clint's resentment rain down on her, hoping it would roll off, knowing it would leave its mark instead.

"He wasn't just washing out underwear and socks in those laundries of his."

"What do you mean?"

"Money! He was laundering money! Thousands. Tens of thousands. Maybe millions over the years."

Jocelyn stared at him. She was trying to reconcile the quarters that run a washing machine or dryer and the amounts of money Clint was talking about. "How could that be?" she asked, hearing how bewildered she sounded.

"Investment," Clint almost shouted. "You put money in. You take it out. You get a loan. You pay it back. You keep moving it from one place to the other."

Jocelyn shook her head. She didn't know what to say. She was shocked, but she was also quite the opposite. In reality, she did not find it hard to believe that Philip could have been involved in something crooked. He had always scoffed at people who had what he referred to as "too many scruples." It would also be just like him to use a chain of laundries for laundering money. He would have found that amusing.

"I don't know all of the ins and outs and details of just how he went about it," Clint was saying. "The police will have to ferret that out eventually. But there is one thing I do know."

He paused, and Jocelyn couldn't help but urge him on. If there was something he was certain of, she wanted to hear what it was because she couldn't be certain of anything right now.

"What is it that you know?" she asked.

"I know that my brother didn't have anything to do with any of this. He was set up."

At that moment, the glass doors slid open behind Clint. A hand pushed the drapes aside to reveal Deputy Roemer standing in the doorway. "I'm beginning to think you may be right about that, Conti" was all he said before Clint stepped out of the way to let him in.

Roemer told them that he had checked the autopsy reports on Philip's death. He'd had to go to Onondaga County to do that since that was where Philip's plane went down. What he had discovered was that there had been no autopsy. The explosion of Philip's plane had been so violent that there was little left to examine as far as human remains were concerned. The skull and jaw fragments were too small or nonexistent to compare with dental records.

Jocelyn cringed to hear that. She had been told such details at the time of Philip's death, but they had not really sunk in then. She hadn't let herself think about them since. Not until now.

"Why were you interested in seeing my husband's autopsy report?" she asked.

"Well, ma'am, it's like this," the deputy drawled. "We have no way of proving anything without those records. But, considering the pattern of deception we are finding, there's sufficient reason to suspect that Mr. Wald's plane crash could have been a continuation of that pattern."

"What do you mean?' Jocelyn's heart was fluttering again.

"I mean that it's reasonable to suspect that your husband isn't dead, after all."

"Oh, my God," Jocelyn breathed.

She sank back against the sofa cushions and put her hand to her face as if to make certain she was still here and real in the midst of so much unreality. She wanted to ask the deputy for more information, but her mind was too stunned to form a question before his beeper began pulsing. He turned it off and excused himself to go to his patrol car and use the radio. Jocelyn nodded acknowledgment without being totally aware of what he had said.

"Jocelyn, are you all right?"

She looked up to find Clint bending over her looking worried.

"I'm just trying to sort this out," she said.

"Yes. I know."

He sounded somber. The weight of all the things they weren't saying encumbered the air between them. Whatever else was there—secret agendas, truths withheld—they had feelings for each other. They had made love and meant it. Where did all of that stand if Philip was, in fact, alive? There was no time even to begin answering that before Deputy Roemer came back in.

"I thought you should know that I have a report of an assault on your friend Hildy Hammond down at the old stone quarry. I'm on my way there now. You can come along if you want."

Jocelyn felt like she was reeling from a one-two punch. Luckily, Clint stepped in.

"I'll drive her there," he said.

The deputy nodded and was gone. In Jocelyn's mind, a voice kept repeating, *What next? What next? What next?* She didn't want to hear what the answer to that might be.

Chapter Fifteen

The rescue squad ambulance beat Jocelyn and Clint to the quarry, so they headed for the hospital. Hildy had been gurneyed directly into a curtained cubicle in the emergency room. Two white-coated physicians and as many nurses moved in and out. Clint used his personal acquaintance with the rescue squad volunteers to find out that there was the possibility of a serious head injury. That was why so much attention was being paid by the medical staff.

"Could her injury have been caused by a fall?" Jocelyn asked.

"Apparently not," Clint said. "According to the ambulance driver, this is one of those blunt-instrument situations."

Jocelyn stared blankly at him.

"As in, she was hit on the head with a blunt instrument."

"Oh, of course."

Jocelyn didn't apologize for being slow on the uptake. She felt as if she had been hit on the head herself, several times. She wasn't sure she had the capacity at this point to assimilate one additional piece of shocking information. Yet, she had to find out what happened to Hildy and whether there could be any truth to Jocelyn's crazy notion that all of these startling pieces fit together somehow into a single picture.

The three volunteer rescuers were still hanging around near the emergency entrance drinking coffee from paper cups. Jocelyn made the approach this time instead of Clint.

"I'm a friend of Miss Hammond's," she said to the trio in general. "Was she able to tell you anything about who did this to her?"

The three men looked at each other. One shrugged, and the other two snickered.

"She told us about it, all right," the man standing closest to Jocelyn said.

He was smirking in a fairly unpleasant way. There was a large greasy stain beneath the embroidered lettering that identified him as a member of the Lewis County Rescue Squad.

"What did Miss Hammond tell you?" Jocelyn spoke solemnly, hoping that would discourage what she considered their inappropriate amusement over Hildy's condition.

"She told us that a ghost attacked her," the man with the stained shirt said.

He looked around at his two companions for confirmation. They mirrored his broad grin in response. Even without the three concurring, Jocelyn would not have doubted the truth of what they reported.

"She called it a spirit," one of the other volunteers added as he crushed his cup in his red-knuckled fist. "She told us it came out of the ground and attacked her. She said that over and over as if she could get us to believe a story like that."

The other two nodded agreement first, then shook their heads to emphasize their skepticism.

"It takes all kinds," the stained shirt said and roused himself from his slouch to move toward the door.

"Sure does."

Jocelyn didn't notice which one of them said that. She was worried about Hildy, frightened by what had happened to her—whatever *had* happened to her—and frustrated by how many unanswered questions she had. These clowns weren't helping matters. She walked away.

JOCELYN INSISTED on going to visit DeDe Mapes. Clint had not been enthusiastic, but when Jocelyn proposed picking up her car and going on her own he agreed to take her. DeDe deserved to know what Deputy Roemer had said. If there was any chance that Philip could be alive, DeDe would be as strongly affected as Jocelyn, maybe even more so. DeDe had loved Philip, very likely she still did. Jocelyn wasn't certain what she had felt for him—gratitude, the kinship of a shared history, some affection. She had thought that added up to love. She'd had nothing to compare it with, until now.

When they reached the Mapes farm, DeDe was standing on the porch, leaning against the rail. She almost seemed to be waiting for them, as if she knew they were coming and that they would tell her something unsettling. She had that deliberately calm look about her that some people get when they anticipate a shock and have resolved to be ready for it. She took a seat in one of the porch rockers and directed Jocelyn to the other. Clint remained at the top of the porch steps while Jocelyn told DeDe what the deputy had said about Philip.

DeDe stared out across the treetops toward the distant sliver of Lake Ontario glimmering on the horizon. The sun must have been shining on that faraway water, though clouds had begun settling in here over Tug Hill. She took a long moment to consider what she had heard before answering.

"I've known Butch Roemer just about since kindergarten," she said at last. "That's the way it is around here. Those of us who stick around been watching each other pretty much all our lives. Was a time Butch did a lot of watching me. As a matter of fact, I paid him some attention myself. Might of paid him more if Reggie hadn't come along."

She paused again, and Jocelyn wondered if she should say something to move the conversation back to the subject at hand. She decided against it. DeDe was as careful a person as most northern New Yorkers. Taking care meant taking time to look at all sides of a question.

"I know Butch Roemer as well as anybody," DeDe went on eventually, "well enough to say that he's smart enough to be right about most things." DeDe turned to look directly and steadily into Jocelyn's eyes. "But Butch is wrong this time. Reggie is dead. I know that for a fact."

"How do you know?" Jocelyn asked, thinking that DeDe might have some bit of evidence no one else was aware of.

DeDe sighed. "If it took me ten minutes to talk you into having faith in my blister cure, then it'll take forever to convince you of this one."

"Try me." Jocelyn felt as if she could be ready to believe just about anything that might explain what was going on here.

"It's like this," DeDe began. "Reggie's dead, but he isn't gone. Not entirely, at least."

Jocelyn's hopes for an explanation fell so hard and suddenly that she could feel them drop.

"If you're going to disbelieve me straight off the bat like that," DeDe said, "what's the use of my telling you anything?"

Jocelyn's face must have revealed what was in her heart. What DeDe had just said sounded like more mumbo jumbo of Jocelyn's mother's variety. Yet, Jocelyn knew DeDe to be a levelheaded, intelligent, independent young woman. Jocelyn nodded to show DeDe she was ready to listen, at least.

DeDe nodded back. "I'd have my doubts, too, if I were you. But living out here makes a person more open to things that might strike you as impossible somewhere else. Maybe it's that so many folks struggled to the death trying to make a life in this place." Her gaze swept over the desolate expanse of Tug Hill from the Mapes hillside to the horizon. "Even back to the Indians, folks have been leaving their bones in this ground. There's lots of spirits on the wind out here, so they say. There was a wind the first night Reggie came back to see me."

"You're talking about his coming back since the plane crash, aren't you?" Jocelyn asked quietly.

"Just a couple of weeks after was the first time," DeDe said. "But don't be thinking it could have been Reggie in the flesh making out he was a ghost. It wasn't like that. I couldn't see him like I see you. It was more that I could feel him, all around me."

"Like being engulfed by the presence of someone or something," Jocelyn said, half to herself. She was thinking about her experience in the quarry, and about

Hildy's description of what happened to her at the dig site and about the sound of a flute playing "Greensleeves."

"That's right," DeDe cried out. "You said it just perfect. Engulfed. That's what I was. He was all around me, even through me. And I know enough about what it's like to be close to Reggie to recognize the feeling."

"I imagine you might know even more about that than I do," Jocelyn said.

"I'm sorry." DeDe reached out and grabbed Jocelyn's hand. "I didn't mean any disrespect. I know you were his wife, and I wasn't."

"I don't take it as disrespect," Jocelyn said.

"I also know what it took for you to come here today to tell me what you found out about Reggie. You didn't have to do that, and I want you to know I appreciate it. I also want you to know that sure as I'm sitting here, Reggie is no longer among the living, not as one of us, he isn't. I expect that is something you might need to be sure about."

DeDe looked from Jocelyn to Clint and back before letting go of Jocelyn's hand. Apparently, she had picked up on whatever was going on between Clint and Jocelyn.

"Thanks," Jocelyn said as she stood up from the rocker. "We'll let you know if we find out anything more."

"Bless you for that," DeDe said. She caught Jocelyn's arm as she was walking away. "Be careful. All of the spirits moving around this place these days may not be as friendly as Reggie's."

Jocelyn nodded. She suspected that DeDe was referring to spirits in the flesh this time. Still, Jocelyn could not help being reminded of what Hildy had said about the attack on her. Was there any possibility at all that her attacker could have been a disembodied Philip that didn't happen to be as friendly as DeDe thought? A week ago, Jocelyn would not have been able to entertain such a thought without derision. Now, she was less certain about what might be true and possible, especially out here on this plateau that did sometimes strike her as haunting and maybe even haunted.

Clint had headed down the steps from the porch. Jocelyn was about to follow him when she spotted Davis Mapes just inside the screen door to the house. He had on the same vest Jocelyn remembered from the other day, and his shaggy hair was disheveled as if he might have been sleeping before the talking on the porch disturbed him. What he said next, however, indicated that he had actually been eavesdropping on the conversation.

"My sister isn't putting you on," he said. "She really does mean what she's saying. If she thought there was a chance you were right about old Reggie still being alive and kicking, she'd blow her top sky-high right now. There's no way she'd sit still for him doing that to her. I can tell you this for a fact."

Jocelyn remembered the rage on DeDe's face that first day she chased the Lincoln out on the road near here. She had a hot temper, all right. Davis was probably correct in his judgment of what she would do if she thought Philip had betrayed her.

"Besides," Davis was saying, "she's always been one to know about haunts and stuff. Our grandma used to say old DeDe had a little bit of witch in her. A sensitive is what Grandma used to call her."

"Quiet down, Davis," DeDe said. "They don't want to hear any of that hill talk. You get back to minding the stand."

Davis shrugged and pushed open the screen door. He sauntered past Jocelyn and Clint and off toward the path that led down the hillside.

"Don't pay any attention to him," DeDe said. "Davis just likes to needle people till he gets a rise out of them. Half the time he doesn't have the first idea what he's talking about."

Jocelyn couldn't help wondering which half of the time this was.

THE FARTHER they got away from the Mapes place, the more outlandish DeDe's story seemed. By the time they reached Tranquility, Jocelyn was just about convinced that living so long in such a remote location must have made DeDe a bit morbid in her preoccupations. Still, Jocelyn could not deny the creeping sensation that prickled the back of her neck when she thought about Philip, either in body or spirit, possibly wandering around these parts. That eerie feeling might have explained her inviting Clint into her trailer and asking if he would like to stay for supper. It was getting on toward that time of day. Jocelyn could certainly face the evening, even the darkness, alone, but she had to admit that she would prefer not to.

They had stopped at the campground office on the way in and called the hospital. Hildy's condition was stabilized. She didn't appear to have suffered a serious head injury, after all. She was sleeping peacefully now, and the doctors wanted her to rest. The nurse suggested that Jocelyn hold off on visiting until the next day. She had to admit she was tired, and traveling back to the hospital tonight would have been a strain. Clint would probably be willing to drive her there, but the thought of sitting next to him in the falling darkness made her nervous.

Jocelyn believed what Clint had said about his motives in singling her out for attention at first. The scandal involving Patrick Conti was linked to Philip's Wash and Dry business. She still wasn't clear on exactly how. Clint was trying to clear his brother's name. That was a worthy and understandable reason for being less than completely forthright in this situation. She even believed that Clint's emotions had gotten in the way of his original purpose eventually. On the other hand, she wasn't sure what she could or should believe about their future together, if in fact any future together was possible.

Jocelyn didn't want to risk the intimacy of Clint's truck cab while that question was still running around in her head. She didn't want to be alone right now, either. Hildy was obviously not available for companionship. Sonny's campsite looked deserted. The Delaneys had their hands full with the campground store and other business. Jocelyn didn't know any of her other neighbors well enough to feel comfortable about inviting herself over for the evening. That left Clint, no matter how conflicted she might feel about being with him.

She decided that the secret was to keep him occupied outside the confined space of the trailer as much as possible. She set him to building a charcoal fire in the covered barbecue grill. It wasn't really necessary for him to watch the coals after he lit them. She instructed him to do so, anyway, and he went along with that.

Maybe he sensed her skittishness about being alone with him. Maybe he felt the same way himself.

After all, why should he get involved in somebody's life that was as mixed up as hers had turned out to be? Why not simply back off and wait until a less complicated prospect came along? She couldn't blame him if he did.

Meanwhile, she kept the minutes moving as normally as possible through the supper preparations and sitting down to eat. She did insist that they eat outdoors despite the thickening cloud cover. The dinette area inside the trailer was even more intimate than Clint's truck cab would have been. She kept the conversation from growing too intimate as well by encouraging Clint to talk about his life as a boy growing up in the north country.

In the beginning, he was hesitant. Then he began talking about himself and Patrick. The anecdotes were tinged with sadness at first, but gradually the humor in them took over as Clint got caught up in the tales of his youthful escapades with the brother who had been his best friend. Jocelyn could almost see the tension easing out of Clint, as if the sinews that had held his powerful shoulders extra taut from the moment she met him might be relaxing now, a notch less strained with every boyhood recollection.

Jocelyn found herself relaxing, as well. She smiled at his stories of adolescent pranks and coming-of-age exploits. Clint's growing-up years had been as carefree as hers had been fraught with worry and responsibility. She had been forced to become an adult way too soon. He had been blessed with the years of being truly young that every child deserves. He shared those years with her so openly that she seemed almost to be living them herself. She heard her own laughter bubbling out of her, and it sounded like the laughter of a girl.

The sky had darkened around them, without her hardly noticing it, except that Clint had gone inside for two hurricane candles. Their golden light flickered on his face. She heard the drops of rain tapping the striped umbrella under which they sat but paid them little mind. Her attention was totally absorbed in Clint. Then she heard something else that she absolutely could not ignore. Clint had stopped to listen, too.

"Do you hear it?" she asked in a whisper between the tripping beats of her heart. She wasn't sure what she wanted him to reply.

"Yes," he said.

Jocelyn released a sigh. She wasn't having auditory hallucinations, after all. But what did that mean? Why would anybody be out here on yet another rainy evening playing "Greensleeves" on a flute? At least, this meant that Clint wasn't the phantom musician. She was relieved to know that.

The music was moving away from them, toward the road that led to the highway. Jocelyn jumped up from the table and hurried down the steps from the deck. She took off at a run in the direction of the musical notes, which grew more distant by the moment. The rain was soft and warm, with none of the fury of the night she had heard the flute before. She ran through the drops without feeling them. She stopped to peer into the darkness ahead but could see nothing. The flute player had too much of a head start. Jocelyn turned back and ran toward the trailer. Clint had been hurrying after her. She encountered him on her dash back up the hill.

"Come with me," she gasped, nearly out of breath. "I think I know where he's going."

She didn't explain further as she ran past Clint toward the Lincoln. He hesitated a moment, then followed.

IT WAS STILL RAINING when they reached the quarry, though not as violently as on that other night here. The clouds hovered just above the ridge. The earth there would be wet but not running mud. Hildy's dig site would be protected by the rock shelf overhang. There would be no such protection for Jocelyn, but it wasn't the rain she was worried about. That's why she was glad Clint had come along. She turned to make certain he was right behind her before stepping onto the rock floor of the quarry. She remembered too vividly what had happened the last time, how she had come close to being sucked into the vortex of a force way beyond her control.

"You lead the way. I'll follow," Clint said softly.

She could barely hear him because the breeze had escalated into a wind. She wondered at that for a moment, whether there could be wind only here and nowhere else. The night air had been calm before they walked through the quarry entrance. Jocelyn shrugged such thoughts away, determined not to let this place spook her.

Speaking of spooks, the flute was no longer audible. All the same, Jocelyn was positive the flute player must be here. An instinct more deeply ingrained than logic told her that. She must have inherited some of her mother's much acclaimed psychic power, after all. Jocelyn felt she had been led to this place as surely as if someone or something had put her on a leash and pulled her here. She didn't know why she had been brought here or what she would find, but she knew somehow that questions could be answered tonight. She only wished her guide had chosen an earlier hour, when there would have been more light, for revelations.

Darkness had fallen, deepened by the low, thick clouds. There was no moon visible, and the large clumps of shrubbery that covered the quarry floor were hulking shapes awaiting her like an army of shadows. Jocelyn had the one flashlight. She shone it on those shapes to dispel the dread they made her feel. She looked behind her again. Clint was a silhouette bigger than any bush, and that encouraged her to press on.

The quarry floor should have felt more solid and substantial than the wet ground that preceded it. Jocelyn told herself that the plates of rock were not shifting beneath her feet, that it was all in her imagination. She was reminded of some geological program she must have seen on television, about shelves moving at the molten heart of the earth and faults opening in the crust with everything from the surface tumbling down and lost. She'd had nightmares after seeing that, much like those of her childhood years when the precariousness of life with her mother had its nighttime expression in unsettling dreams.

The disturbing recollections were not so easy to shrug off, but she did her best. She heard Clint brush against some brambles behind her. Twigs snapped, and he made a low muttering sound that reminded her she was not alone. If she was to be tumbled into the core of the earth, Clint would tumble with her. That reassurance gave her the impetus to pick up speed and move steadily across the quarry floor toward the back wall and Hildy's dig site. Jocelyn kept the light trained low to the ground rather than shining it straight where it might telegraph their approach. Something was out there, and she shouldn't let it know she was coming.

She heard that something before she saw it, a chinking sound that made her think of Jacob Marley's ghost clanking his chains in the Dickens classic. A chill ran through her as she heard the chinking sound again, closer now because she had moved toward it. She was headed straight for it, whatever it was. She ducked behind a clump of shrubbery and looked back just in time to see Clint's crouching form do the same. He looked smaller bent over like that in the dark. She wished she could check with him to make certain he had heard the same thing she did, but they were too close now to take the chance. If she could hear that chinking sound, whatever was making it would be able to hear her too.

Jocelyn inched along among the bushes. The more open trail was too risky. She wished she could see where she was going. She decided to take a small chance. She straightened up enough to see through the thin upper branches of the shrubbery. There was a light ahead, a soft glow muted and diffused by the rain and cloudy darkness. She couldn't see anything besides that glow. She snapped off her own light and listened for the chinking sound, which continued more regularly now.

There was the sound of falling rain, as well, gentle touches of hundreds of droplets against twigs and leaves all across the quarry. That soothing symphony was accompanied by the sweet pungent scent of earth and greenery opened wide to the moisture and drinking it in. Jocelyn might have been lulled by the soft and gentle night if it hadn't been for that chinking sound. A shovel hitting rock. Somebody was digging at Hildy's excavation. Jocelyn was sure of it.

She turned to beckon Clint forward in the darkness. She had to communicate this to him somehow, perhaps in a whisper so low it couldn't be heard above the raindrops. In that instant, she noticed that there was no wind any longer. Here, deep into the quarry, there was only hush and quiet rain patter, as if the wind resided only at the mouth of the quarry like a sentinel on guard. Jocelyn didn't like that thought any better than she had its creepy predecessors. Unfortunately, she couldn't seem to shake the feeling that she was in a bewitched place.

She strained to find Clint in the darkness and breathed a sigh of relief as his crouched form emerged from behind nearby branches and eased toward her. She couldn't see his features through the gloom. It wasn't until he was right behind her that she knew something was wrong. Dampness magnifies scent, just as it had the smell of the earth and foliage. The odor it was magnifying from the person behind her was recognizable, but not because she associated it with Clint.

Motor oil! She was smelling motor oil!

She lifted her flashlight to strike just as a grip caught her arm. She struggled, but she was too off-center in her bent-down position to make much impact. The person holding her wasn't as big as Clint, but big enough to overpower Jocelyn, especially when she was taken by surprise. The flashlight fell from her hand as he clenched her wrist in a painful twist.

"Give it up, lady," a vaguely familiar voice growled in her ear. "You should've known enough to stay in out of the rain tonight because you're in big trouble now."

He stood up and pulled her with him. She still couldn't place the voice.

"Who are you?" she asked.

"I suppose it doesn't matter what you know. You and your boyfriend aren't getting out of here alive. I'm Charlie Gillis. From the airport. You remember me?"

"The mechanic who worked on Philip's plane."

"You got it, honey." He laughed unpleasantly as he dragged her by the arm onto the path. "The best mechanic around. Good enough to rig a crash and explosion so there ain't enough left to investigate and nobody can tell it was anything but an accident."

The chinking sound had stopped. As Gillis pulled Jocelyn along toward the dig site, she could see that the light had been put out, as well. She tried not to think about what it could mean that Philip's plane had been engineered to crash.

"Turn the lights back on," Gillis called out. "It's me, and I've got the snoopers taken care of."

"Are you sure?"

Jocelyn knew who that voice belonged to even before the light was snapped back on to reveal Sonny Shannon with a shovel in his hand.

"I'm sure," Gillis said. "I knocked Conti out on his way in here. Conked him so hard he may not wake up till next week. I found this one hiding in the bushes."

Behind Sonny, a hole had been dug into the earthen wall of the quarry. They were actually a few yards away from Hildy's site. Within the new excavation a large sack crusted with mud was visible.

Sonny followed her gaze to the sack. An ugly grin broke across his dirt-smudged face. "Your better half," he said, jerking his head toward the hole in the quarry wall. "Right where I planted him last year."

"Philip?" Jocelyn asked in disbelief.

"That's right," Sonny said, still grinning. "Good old Philip or Reggie or whatever you want to call him.

He's been croaked all of this time, after all. Not till a couple of weeks after you thought he was. But croaked is croaked no matter when it happens.''

"How did he die?'' Jocelyn asked, feeling suddenly cold and numb, as if she had been newly struck with the shock of Philip's death all over again.

"Charlie here and I gave him an assist to his final reward.''

"Yeah,'' Charlie said, shoving Jocelyn forward into the light. "Too bad we assisted him a little too soon.''

"Shut up,'' Sonny blurted out.

"What's the matter?'' Gillis sneered. "Don't you want the lady to know how you screwed up?''

"Shut up, I said.''

"If I got the big boys down on our necks like you did by wasting her old man before we found where he hid their money, I wouldn't want nobody to know about it, either.''

"That was an accident. How was I supposed to know his heart would give out before I got him to talk?''

"Our big-city friends pay you to know stuff like that,'' Charlie said. "They don't pay you to be a screw-up.''

Sonny dropped the shovel and lunged forward. He was holding a gun. Maybe he had it all along, in the other hand from the shovel. Jocelyn hadn't noticed, but now she was noticing everything.

Sonny's attention was on Gillis. Gillis's grip on her arm had loosened slightly as he prepared to defend himself. The shovel was too far away for Jocelyn to get to in time. But there was a pick angled into the crevice beneath the muddy sack, and the dirt around it was crumbly from the rain.

Jocelyn yanked her arm out of Gillis's grasp and leaped at the pick, all in one motion. That split second of surprise was all she needed. She meant to grab the pick from the loose earth and knock Sonny out with it. Instead, pulling the pick free dislodged the sack, as well. It came toppling down, straight onto Sonny. He fell and lay very still.

Jocelyn had time only to deduce that his head must have hit a rock. At that moment, Gillis dived toward her across Sonny's prone form. She lifted the pick, knowing Gillis could be too close for her to strike him full force. She braced for a struggle. Then Gillis sprawled over the sack and dropped like a stone at her feet.

She stepped back and stared down at him, her pick poised to attack should he try to get up again. He lay as still as Sonny. Had Gillis tripped over the sack?

"He should have known this square head of mine was too hard for that tap he gave me."

Clint stood over Gillis. The lantern cast light upward on Clint's face, just as the campfire had the first night she saw him. She couldn't see his deep-set eyes tonight, either, but this time she had no doubt they were smiling.

Epilogue

Jocelyn had driven down the road to the Mapes vegetable stand this morning, just as she had the afternoon she first arrived in the north country. This time she found the place on purpose, not by accident. She and Clint were here to help DeDe and her brothers pack up and move to the house she and Philip had shared. Jocelyn had deeded it to DeDe the day before.

Sonny Shannon and Charlie Gillis had been transferred from the county jail to a federal lockup. They were taken in on the charges of Sonny's attack on Hildy and Charlie's break-in at Jocelyn's trailer. Charlie was also suspected of having shot at Clint and Jocelyn that day at the flea market. Now they were in even more serious trouble, to be tried for conspiracy to murder and monetary fraud among other things.

They had admitted to framing Patrick Conti who had begun investigating Reggie Williams on his own. Sonny had planted the counterfeit bills to implicate Patrick and lead the investigation away from the money-laundering scheme that was really going on. Exhumation of Patrick's body would reveal the drugs in his system that Sonny had planted in his coffee mug just before Patrick took off on his last, tragic ride.

Patrick's name had been cleared of any connection with wrongdoing, and he was to be publicly exonerated and given a posthumous ceremony as a police hero.

Neither Sonny nor Charlie had as yet named their New York City contacts. Those contacts weren't the kind of people who liked being ratted on, and their information sources seemed to be everywhere. That's how they had found out that Philip planned his own supposed death in the plane that exploded with a small-time hood on board after Philip parachuted to safety. Charlie and Sonny had been only too eager to track Philip down and pay him back for using them the way he had.

Meanwhile, the money Philip skimmed from his laundering operation had not been found. Jocelyn had been watched for months, even back in Syracuse, in case she might know its whereabouts. They had searched her trailer looking for clues. Nobody seemed to know where the stash of cash might be—except that Clint had made some broad hints to DeDe about checking a patch of fairly new masonry he had noticed in the rear cellar wall of the house she was moving into today. As far as anyone else knew, Philip had taken the location of the money to the grave with him because of Sonny's blundering.

"So, I'm the reason the house of cards finally toppled?" Hildy asked. She was here more as reigning temporary invalid, complete with head bandage, than as moving-day helper.

"That's right," Davis Mapes said. "Sonny thought that old quarry would've been filled in a long time ago. Then you threw a monkey wrench in the works and got the construction stopped. When you started digging around in there, he was sure you'd find Reggie where he'd stashed him." Davis looked suddenly sheepish. "Sorry, ma'am," he said to Jocelyn. "Somebody ought to stash my big mouth somewhere."

"Ain't that the truth," Dolby chimed in. He was looking much less sullen today than when Jocelyn last saw him.

"That's all right," she said. "Philip is past history for me now. I've put him to rest, and I think he's put himself to rest, too." Along with a certain flute melody, she thought to herself. "I'm concentrating on the future these days."

"And I'll bet you won't take any side roads the next time you feel like doing some camping in the north country," Clint said. He put down the packing box he had been carrying and slipped his arm around Jocelyn.

She looked up at the strong-featured face she had grown to love and smiled. "No detours," she said. "From now on, I take the most direct route there is—straight to you."

Take 4 bestselling love stories FREE

Plus get a FREE surprise gift!

Fifty red-blooded, white-hot, true-blue hunks
from every State in the Union!

Look for MEN MADE IN AMERICA! Written by some of
our most popular authors, these stories feature fifty of
the strongest, sexiest men, each from a different state in
the union!

Two titles available every other month at your favorite
retail outlet.

In March, look for:

TANGLED LIES by Anne Stuart (Hawaii)
ROGUE'S VALLEY by Kathleen Creighton (Idaho)

In April, look for:

LOVE BY PROXY by Diana Palmer (Illinois)
POSSIBLES by Lass Small (Indiana)

You won't be able to resist MEN MADE IN AMERICA!

HARLEQUIN®

Don't miss these Harlequin favorites by some of our most distinguished authors!
And now, you can receive a discount by ordering two or more titles!

HT#25409	THE NIGHT IN SHINING ARMOR by JoAnn Ross	$2.99 ☐
HT#25471	LOVESTORM by JoAnn Ross	$2.99 ☐
HP#11463	THE WEDDING by Emma Darcy	$2.89 ☐
HP#11592	THE LAST GRAND PASSION by Emma Darcy	$2.99 ☐
HR#03188	DOUBLY DELICIOUS by Emma Goldrick	$2.89 ☐
HR#03248	SAFE IN MY HEART by Leigh Michaels	$2.89 ☐
HS#70464	CHILDREN OF THE HEART by Sally Garrett	$3.25 ☐
HS#70524	STRING OF MIRACLES by Sally Garrett	$3.39 ☐
HS#70500	THE SILENCE OF MIDNIGHT by Karen Young	$3.39 ☐
HI#22178	SCHOOL FOR SPIES by Vickie York	$2.79 ☐
HI#22212	DANGEROUS VINTAGE by Laura Pender	$2.89 ☐
HI#22219	TORCH JOB by Patricia Rosemoor	$2.89 ☐
HAR#16459	MACKENZIE'S BABY by Anne McAllister	$3.39 ☐
HAR#16466	A COWBOY FOR CHRISTMAS by Anne McAllister	$3.39 ☐
HAR#16462	THE PIRATE AND HIS LADY by Margaret St. George	$3.39 ☐
HAR#16477	THE LAST REAL MAN by Rebecca Flanders	$3.39 ☐
HH#28704	A CORNER OF HEAVEN by Theresa Michaels	$3.99 ☐
HH#28707	LIGHT ON THE MOUNTAIN by Maura Seger	$3.99 ☐

Harlequin Promotional Titles

#83247	YESTERDAY COMES TOMORROW by Rebecca Flanders	$4.99 ☐
#83257	MY VALENTINE 1993	$4.99 ☐
	(short-story collection featuring Anne Stuart, Judith Arnold, Anne McAllister, Linda Randall Wisdom)	

(limited quantities available on certain titles)

	AMOUNT	$
DEDUCT:	10% DISCOUNT FOR 2+ BOOKS	$
ADD:	POSTAGE & HANDLING	$
	($1.00 for one book, 50¢ for each additional)	
	APPLICABLE TAXES*	$ _____
	TOTAL PAYABLE	$ _____
	(check or money order—please do not send cash)	

To order, complete this form and send it, along with a check or money order for the total above, payable to Harlequin Books, to: **In the U.S.:** 3010 Walden Avenue, P.O. Box 9047, Buffalo, NY 14269-9047; **In Canada:** P.O. Box 613, Fort Erie, Ontario, L2A 5X3.

Name: _____

Address: _____ City: _____

State/Prov.: _____ Zip/Postal Code: _____

*New York residents remit applicable sales taxes.
Canadian residents remit applicable GST and provincial taxes.

HBACK-JM

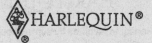

HARLEQUIN®

COMING SOON TO
A STORE NEAR YOU...

THE MAIN
ATTRACTION

By *New York Times* Bestselling Author

This March, look for THE MAIN ATTRACTION by popular
author Jayne Ann Krentz.

Ten years ago, Filomena Cromwell had left her small town
in shame. Now she is back determined to get her sweet,
sweet revenge....

Soon she has her ex-fiancé, who cheated on her with
another woman, chasing her all over town. And he isn't
the only one. Filomena lets Trent Ravinder catch her.

Can she control the fireworks she's set into motion?

When the only time you have for yourself is...

Spring into spring—by giving yourself a March Break! Take a few *stolen moments* and treat yourself to a Great Escape. Relax with one of our brand-new stories (or with all six!).

Each STOLEN MOMENTS title in our Great Escapes collection is a complete and never-before-published *short* novel. These contemporary romances are 96 pages long—the perfect length for the busy woman of the nineties!

Look for Great Escapes in our Stolen Moments display this March!

SIZZLE by Jennifer Crusie
ANNIVERSARY WALTZ
by Anne Marie Duquette
MAGGIE AND HER COLONEL
by Merline Lovelace
PRAIRIE SUMMER by Alina Roberts
THE SUGAR CUP by Annie Sims
LOVE ME NOT by Barbara Stewart

Wherever Harlequin and Silhouette books are sold.

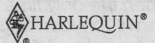

HARLEQUIN®

Harlequin proudly presents four stories about *convenient* but not *conventional* reasons for marriage:

- ◆ To save your godchildren from a "wicked stepmother"

- ◆ To help out your eccentric aunt—and her sexy business partner

- ◆ To bring an old man happiness by making him a grandfather

- ◆ To escape from a ghostly existence and become a real woman

Marriage By Design—four brand-new stories by four of Harlequin's most popular authors:

CATHY GILLEN THACKER
JASMINE CRESSWELL
GLENDA SANDERS
MARGARET CHITTENDEN

Don't miss this exciting collection of stories about marriages of convenience. Available in April, wherever Harlequin books are sold.

MBD94